Young and Reckless
Part I

A Novel

Khaaliq Binns

Published and Distributed by:
The Creator Publishing
P.O. Box 451665
Los Angeles, CA 90045
Email: belectrical41@yahoo.com

Cover design by Jay DeVance III
First printing February 2014
978-0-615-96559-8
Library of Congress Control Number 2014937520
10987654321

ACKNOWLEDGMENTS

To my father, Don Binns, thank you for your unconditional love. You are the greatest father in the world; I am blessed to have you for a father.

To all my family members, thanks for all that you have done to encourage me.

To all my homies, you are too many to name and you know who you are. Thank you for the role that you have played in my life.

To Dr. Rosie Milligan, thank you so much for evaluating my literary work and encouraging me to go forward with my literary endeavor.

FOREWORD

The streets of South Central Los Angeles have not changed since crack cocaine was introduced as a hustle in the early '80s. But Sean, aka Scrilla, takes his street hustles to a different level after investing in a well-known strip club in Los Angeles, and embarks on human trafficking overseas beautiful women, with a crew of young thugs on his payroll to kill at will, manipulating them to absorb more street power, and financial gain until they crack the code of the truth about Scrilla and introduce him to a deadly game of Urban War after their currency grows within their new clique called the U-Mob, known as the Unforgiven Mobsters.

CHAPTER 1

The South Central Los Angeles morning air was thin and chilly at 4:00 A.M. Ms. Francis looked at the time on the gold watch on her left, frail wrist, while she waited behind the three-hundred-pound, dark-skinned, baldheaded security guard, watching as their manager opened the back door to Nix's Check Cashing's cemented building. The security guard took a sip of his coffee from the Krispy Kreme donut Styrofoam cup before checking the safety button on his .45-caliber automatic pistol holstered to his waist.

The back door opened slowly as the manager, Mr. Jameson, looked around nervously before he entered the financial business. As soon as his right foot hit the gray-carpeted pavement inside Nix's, he heard Ms. Francis gagging at the mouth and a single gun blast rang out in the air. Mr. Jameson tried to run, but was snatched up by two black masked men.

"Take us to the safe, nigga, and don't play any kind of games, old muthafucka!"

The third masked man ordered the three-hundred-pound security guard to lay face down on the gray carpet in the middle of the business, smashing the barrel of a shotgun to the back of his wrinkly baldhead.

Ms. Francis stood to the side by the front counter attached to a bulletproof glass window with her hands together in a style of prayer, looking down and whispering to herself. The masked man holding the shotgun dug in the back pocket of his black khaki pants and tossed an orange plastic Foot Locker shopping bag to Ms. Francis, hitting her in the face.

"Start unlocking them drawers on the counter. You got one minute to stuff that bag to the top!"

Ms. Francis adjusted her glasses on her face, dug in her cotton brown trench coat for the keys to the counters and commenced to opening the drawers, filling the bag with new currency bills.

The other two masked men that marched Mr. Jameson to the safe came from the back room, carrying stuffed plastic Foot Locker bags with their glock-automatic pistols. The tallest of the masked man yelled to the top of his lungs. "Let's go!"

Before leaving out the back door, the tall masked man stopped by the security guard and instructed Ms. Francis and Mr. Jameson to lie face down beside the comatose security guard, and tied their hands behind their backs with duct tape. Then, he retrieved a .357 Revolver from the security guard's holster before tying his wrists with duct tape.

The three robbers ran out the back door into the morning air. Jumping over a brick wall, where a burgundy 1986 Monte Carlo Luxury Sport idling on a Dunkin Donuts parking lot, the robbers snatched their masks from their faces before jumping into the old school automobile, and pulling off with the back tires on the chrome twenty-four-inch rims screeching and burning rubber.

Demetrius, aka Meech, raced the 454 engine under the hood of the Luxury Sport down Slauson Boulevard, making a right turn and zigzagging through the back streets until he made it home, listening to sirens echoing through the neighborhood.

Six minutes later, LAPD officers were crawling around the crime scene of Nix's Check Cashing, writing down reports and checking the building for any evidence or fingerprints. Some officers questioned students that were walking down Slauson Boulevard on their way to high school and people who stood at the bus stops going to work.

A helicopter, known in any urban area as the Ghetto Bird," made itself known in the sky, hovering around the Westside of South Central Los Angeles, looking for the suspects who robbed Nix Check Cashing. By the time the helicopter was completely in the air, Demetrius was pulling the luxury sport inside the garage of his mother's house, cutting off the engine.

CHAPTER 2

Demetrius Williams once had dreams of going to the NBA until he got caught up with the wrong kind of crowd and the wrong lifestyle that was hidden from his mother, Vickie, a forty-two-year-old hard-working black mother who worked at the County building as a caseworker. Demetrius was currently Westchester High School's basketball team prospect in his senior year. He was standing six feet seven inches tall at eighteen years old and was slam-dunking from behind the free-throw line, with numerous college scouts jocking him every game.

Vickie was on her way to work and just stepped out of the bathroom, touching her face up with make-up. Going down the hallway of their three-bedroom home, she stopped by Demetrius' room and knocked on the door.

"Meech, get yo ass up boy and get ready for school!"

"I ain't going!"

Vickie turned the doorknob and pushed open the door. She stood in the middle of the doorway with her right hand planted on the waist of her black dress, eyeing Demetrius while he was laid up under the blankets on his bed with nothing but the wave cap on his head poking out. When he heard his mom enter the room, his face came from under the blankets, facing her.

"What the hell you mean you ain't going to school? I just paid for your prom tickets and pictures. Don't you got to go pick up your tickets to prom today?"

"I ain't going to prom, Momma!"

"Why?"

"I just found out I'm sixty credits short and I ain't graduating, so I ain't celebrating no prom."

"Boy, that ain't no reason to not go to prom. You just got to go to summer school and make up the credits."

Before Vickie could finish lecturing her son, her husband Charles cut her off. Stepping from behind her, looking down at Demetrius while he began to rise from up under the covers.

"Look here, boy! While you living up under me and your mother's roof for free, you gonna go to school, you gonna obey your mother and you gonna talk to your mom with a respectful tone. What the hell you mean, 'I ain't going to school!' If you can't follow some simple life rules, then you can leave, Demetrius."

By the time Charles was done talking, Demetrius was lacing up his white Air Force 1 sneakers, standing tall in his red basketball shorts facing Charles' six-foot frame with no fear.

"Nigga, you ain't my daddy and this ain't yo house, fool. I don't give a fuck if you help pay the bills; this my mamma shit and you can't tell me to go nowhere, nigga!"

Charles fired to Demetrius face with a sharp right closed fist hook.

Vickie yelled at the top of her lungs when a brawl broke out in the room. "Y'all stop before I call the police! Stop it!"

With a mouthful of blood from Charles's punch, Demetrius held Charles in a headlock, swinging half of his body around the room. Demetrius was trying to knee Charles in the face while he had his head locked in his long arms until he felt a stick beating on his back repeatedly. When the stick beating wouldn't stop, Demetrius unloosed Charles's neck and looked at his mother who was holding a broomstick. Charles was about to attack Demetrius until Vickie shouted.

"Charles, you bet not touch him! Y'all make me sick with all this bullshit."

Demetrius had tears welling up in his brown eyes, looking at Vickie. "Damn, Momma, you just seen this grown ass nigga sock me in the mouth, and you turn around and beat me with a stick for protecting myself! You in love with the dick more than flesh and blood!"

The words that bounced off Demetrius's tongue crushed Vickie's feelings. Charles walked out the room, pulling Vickie by the arm. Demetrius went inside his closet, snatching a few outfits and sneakers out, and he stuffed them inside a trash bag. Then he reached for the phone on his small night dresser by the bed, and dialed a number. While waiting on someone to answer the phone, he opened the top drawer on the night dresser, retrieving a two-toned, chrome and black steel P89 Ruger from under some folded boxers, and loaded a bullet in the chamber.

"Hey, Scrilla, come get me now, dog. I'm at my mom's house. I just had to whoop on her boyfriend."

Twenty minutes after the altercation between Charles and Demetrius jumped off, a black Chrysler 300M, sitting on black rims, pulled up in front of the house while Vickie watched from the living room window, wondering who it was behind the wheel and why they stopped in front of her home. Ten seconds later, Demetrius walked through the living room, holding a bag of clothes wearing a blue LA Dodgers cap to the back of his head, a white t-shirt and blue jeans cuffed over his white Air Force One sneakers. He looked at his mom standing by the living room window while not paying any attention to Charles sitting on the couch looking pissed off.

"I'll be back later to get the rest of my clothes and my car from the garage."

Demetrius stormed out the front door and walked out the front yard, jumping in the passenger side of the Chrysler 300M, after tossing his bag of clothes in the back seat.

Vickie watched her son pull off with a stranger. Still hurt inside, Vickie knew her son was entering a chaotic world, falling into his father's footsteps, but it was nothing she could do anymore. Demetrius was now eighteen years old and she knew if he got into any trouble, he was going to prison and she could no longer save him like in the past when he went to Juvenile Hall jail for car theft.

Vickie got herself together and left for work while Charles turned on the television in the living room, watching the morning breaking news that featured the Nix's Check Cashing robbery with unidentified suspects and a few other unsolved robberies on businesses in the nearby neighborhood that occurred within the last few months.

By noon, Charles had stripped from his construction uniform and had taken a shower. He had the house to himself and used the quietness around him to meditate on the incident that took place with him and Demetrius, regretting that he started the fight by punching him. After Charles got dressed, he rolled up a zig zag filled with marijuana, and walked in the kitchen. He grabbed a can of Miller High Life beer out the refrigerator, cracked it open and took a fat swallow before closing the refrigerator door.

After collecting his thoughts, he decided to call up his friend from work, Big Steve, to invite him over to watch their favorite football team—Dallas Cowboys—in the playoffs and drink a few cold beers.

Stepping out on the back porch to breathe in some fresh air while he waited on Big Steve to show up, Charles reminisced on his younger days as a thug growing up and running the streets of Los Angeles before his redemption took over while he was in prison. He walked to the garage, raised the big wide door and looked at the clean old school Monte Carlo he gave Demetrius for his seventeenth birthday last year. As he moved closer to the car, a puzzled look masked his face. He started to realize how much the car had changed since he gave it to Demetrius. As he walked around it and looked at the interior through the glass windows, he saw that a lot of change was invested in the car and was wondering where the money was coming from, thinking that Demetrius was selling drugs, stealing cars, or pulling robberies. He opened the car door, looked inside and ran his hand across the white and burgundy pinstriped crocodile seats. A chrome "B" and "M" stick shift was mounted down in the burgundy suede carpet, matching the all chrome-plated steering wheel. The car was sitting high in the air on twenty-four-inch chrome Lowen-Hart Rims with a burgundy painted lip touching thin Pirelli Tires. The burgundy paint was wet like a Charms Blow

Pop with graphics running along the sides of the body. When Charles took closed the door, Big Steve was walking through the garage carrying a case of beer and slapped hands with Charles, checking out the Luxury Sport.

"Damn, Charles, this muthafucka clean."

"Say, Big Steve, let me ask you a question. Take a look at the car and let me know how much you think its worth."

It took about fifteen to twenty minutes for Charles to get an answer from Steve. After looking at the chromed-out engine, Big Steve closed the hood. "Shit, Charles, its worth at least twenty grand. Why the hell you put all that money into this old muthafucka when you just could have gotten a used truck or something new?"

"This my stepson's and I ain't put a dime in this car since last year and that was to get some gas to go to work."

"Damn, Charles, where the hell Demetrius work at? I need a job where he employed."

"That's the root of the problem. That little nigga ain't got no job, Big Steve. But his momma don't want to listen. Every time I tell her about him going down the wrong path by letting him smoke weed in his room, she put his basketball in front of my truth, and listen to his lies every night about where he been when he coming in the house two and three in the morning."

In his youth, Charles lived the life of crime as a young gangster, but he wasn't trying to wear out his peace at home by trying to give proper knowledge about life to a juvenile delinquent at the beginning of the adult life.

Charles and Big Steve headed back in the house to catch the Dallas Cowboys game. Before they made it all the way in the house through the back door, several shots rang out and Big Steve almost tripped over the first step on the porch walking behind Charles. They both looked at each other and spoke the same words at the same time, "Tech-Nine."

***

Scrilla and Demetrius were still in the Chrysler 300M, bending corners and making stops here and there. Demetrius was reclined in the passenger seat, with his hat tilted over his eyes, high off purple haze marijuana, thinking about his life, how he just all of a sudden gave up on his basketball dreams and traded them for street dreams. His conscious and natural awareness was talking to him, telling him that he was facing an unfamiliar world that contained all kinds of dangers when he did his first robbery before the Nix Check Cashing robbery. He dozed off while Scrilla was macking to a female about a booty call on his cell phone, and driving around smoking on a blunt.

Scrilla was a hood wizard who knew the ins and outs of the Los Angeles slums. He was from Shreveport, Louisiana and moved to California with his grandmother at the age of thirteen. He never knew his father, and his mother was murdered when he was ten years old. He quickly developed the habit of not depending on other people to protect and shelter him. This meant that in every subsequent encounter in life, in which he felt fear, he could turn only to himself, especially when he first moved to California where he had very little family during the crack cocaine epidemic in the 1980s. His family became street hustlers, Crips and Bloods, and thug-lords who showed love to his street game.

Scrilla watched Demetrius grow up from a little kid riding his bike down the street by where he used to peddle cocaine on the corner, until he made it to high school, walking down the street, dribbling his basketball past Scrilla and bragging to Scrilla about how he would go to the NBA.

Demetrius grew up with little parental supervision and disdain for authority after the LAPD killed his father right in front of him as a child sitting in the backseat of his father's car. His farther, Demetrius Sr., couldn't face a Christmas being broke, with three children by two different women, so he got anxious one Christmas Eve. While on the way to taking Demetrius to elementary school, he tried to rob a bank. However, after he got away with the money, and standing in front of his car, listening to his son crying in the backseat, with a bag of money in one hand and a pistol in the other, he was gunned down right in front of his house when he wouldn't surrender to the cops,

Demetrius felt Scrilla tapping him on the shoulder while he was napping from the strong weed smoke. He looked at Scrilla with lazy eyes.

"Damn, young nigga, you can't handle a little purple smoke, you supposed to be paying attention."

"Yeah, I know. That's some good ass weed, Scrilla."

"So where you want me to drop you off at, young nigga?"

Demetrius got quiet for a second because he knew he didn't have anywhere to go. All he had was $30,000 in cash from his share of the $90,000 from the Nix Check Cashing robbery, a P-89 Ruger and a bag full of clothes and shoes that were in Scrilla's backseat.

"Damn, Scrilla! Fuck it, just take me by my mom's house so I can get my car out the garage and I'll go get a room."

"Say, youngsta, I don't think it's cool to ride around in that donk after it was witnessed in a robbery."

The response that rolled off Scrilla's tongue completely woke up Demetrius from his marijuana slump.

"How the fuck you know that, Scrilla?"

"On the streets, young Meech, somebody's always watchin or either is talkin'. Every morning, after I close my strip club, I stop by Dunkin Donuts to get some coffee as soon as it opens at 4:30 AM sharp. I watched you hit the brick wall with two other niggas and drove off."

"Damn, Scrilla, I'm glad you ain't no snitch and you the only one that saw us."

Scrilla turned the volume down on the car's audio player, letting his Lil Boosie CD play low. He shook his head and blew out weed smoke. Looking at Demetrius, disappointed, he raised his voice.

"Meech, what the fuck is up with you, Dog? What happened with going to the NBA and making your mom's proud? Making me your personal bodyguard, bro, and taking trips overseas, fuckin bad bitches. You rather trade all that just to be an enemy to the public society dog!?"

"I don't give a fuck no more, Scrilla! Either you gon' be my homey or not, because I don't need another father, Dog. Pop's been gone."

"Look, young Meech, I ain't trying to come down hard on you, but this street life is way deeper than you think, young homey."

"I ain't no square ass nigga or no buster ass nigga, Scrill. I can swim with the sharks."

"You still ain't gettin' the picture, young Meech. Don't no street hustler last that long. It's a young man's game. By the time hustlers reach their late twenties, they slow down and something bad happens or they go scurrying into a low-paying job or snitch on the next nigga scared to go to the penitentiary."

Demetrius was blinded and blocked from true reality by the money and the lifestyle he was now living. He didn't go through all the trials and tribulations Scrilla had to go through to survive and make it at the age of thirty-three years old.

They both got quiet as Scrilla pulled up to a red light on Crenshaw Boulevard. Scrilla's street lecture didn't scare Demetrius one ounce. Demetrius caught a thrill flirting with so much danger, but he would soon be awakened to real turf talk. Scrilla drove up Crenshaw, going south until he reached the cross street—Century Boulevard. Lil Webbie's "Made Nigga" song was pumping out the speakers of the Chrysler. Scrilla was spitting down the middle of the Swisher Sweet blunt with his two thumbs while Demetrius was breaking down marijuana buds on a music CD cover.

Scrilla rolled down his window and dumped the guts of the blunt out onto the street. A burnt orange Chevy Avalanche pickup truck swooped up on the side of Scrilla's Chrysler at the red light. As soon as he pulled his arm back in the window, two men, wearing black hooded sweat shirts leaped from the back of the flat bed of the Avalanche, ran up on Scrilla, brandishing pistols.

"Turn the car off, nigga, turn the car off!"

Demetrius slowly tried to slide his right hand in the waistband of his jeans until shots fired after one of the carjackers snatched

Scrilla's thick gold necklace from his neck. A bullet tore through Scrilla's left jaw, leaving a hole in his mouth, while one grazed the top of his head. He ducked his head, reached for the gas pedal and drove the Chrysler through the window of a Shoe Warehouse after running the car up and over the curb on Century Boulevard. The car horn blared from Scrilla's bloody forehead pressed against it after the crash. Demetrius was knocked unconscious in the front seat.

CHAPTER 3

Vickie got a phone call in the middle of the night by Detectives telling her that her son was involved in an attempted carjacking and shooting. She quickly got out of the bed, got dressed and grabbed her car keys. Charles was aroused from sleep by Vickie's sniffling and moving around. He arose from under the covers, wearing nothing but his boxers and a small gold necklace around his neck, rubbing his baldhead.

"Baby, where you going?"

"Demetrius just got shot in the car with someone. I'm going to the hospital."

"Hold on, baby, I'm coming with you."

***

Scrilla had just gotten the giant hole in his jaw stitched up, and bandages on his head and arms. The airbag in the steering wheel saved his life and the bullet wounds were non-life threatening. Demetrius took a bullet to his left thigh, but the car crash had him knocked out since the accident occurred. He was lucky to be alive because of the seatbelt he was wearing. He and Scrilla were housed in different rooms.

When Vickie and Charles finally made it to Cedar Sinai Hospital in Beverly Hills, Demetrius was conscious. He looked up in his mother's watery eyes, saying nothing, with IVs stuck in his arms. Tears ran down her cheeks. She grabbed Demetrius' hand and squeezed it lightly.

"Son…I can't preach to you no more. You done got grown on me and I guess you got to learn the hard way. Your coach wants to talk to you. He said it's important. Demetrius, I just hope you don't get yourself killed in those streets."

"Don't stress off me, Momma, I'll be cool."

"Your sister misses you. Her prom is coming up next weekend."

"I need you to come pick me up when I'm released, Momma."

"Demetrius, I'm going to tell you right now. If you not going to try and finish school to graduate or at least work a job, you can't live with me and that thug-life shit you got going on."

After Vickie and Charles left the hospital, Scrilla was being pushed in a wheelchair by a young beautiful woman named

Stella. She pushed him into Demetrius' room and they all kicked it for about an hour before it was time for Scrilla to check out the hospital. Scrilla had on his hospital gown and slippers. He rolled up beside Demetrius' bed, looked him in the eyes and shook his hand.

"When you get well, young Meech, decide what you gonna do with your life before you come visit me again. I only fuck with niggas that's loyal enough to take a bullet for me and kill for me. If you can do that and keep your mouth quiet when the police question you, then you can roll with me from time to time. If you not ready, stay away from me, dog, and go back to school or whatever else you gonna do, because I almost lost my life rolling with you and you didn't squeeze off one round on those niggas who shot me in the jaw! Now you see why I roll solo. Take care, homey. I'm gone."

The honey brown, long curly-haired female pushed Scrilla out of Demetrius' room, and left the hospital.

Demetrius felt like he let Scrilla down by dozing off on the marijuana they were smoking on that night of the accident after he told him to keep his focus in the rear view mirror. He let the attempted jackers roll right up on them when he had a loaded P-89 Ruger with the safety off ready to pop. He made a promise to himself that he would find the niggas, who took Scrilla's chain, and kill them to gain back his loyalty.

CHAPTER 4

Kamil

Young, black, dangerous, wild, sneaky, conniving, and untrustworthy. Kamil damn near owned up to every category and name Satan's soul possessed in the human form. He was one of Demetrius' friends that participated in the Check Cashing robbery and was the second star player on Westchester's High School basketball team next to Demetrius.

Kamil was treating his $30,000 share of the Nix's Check Cashing robbery like he hit the lottery, spending money like water. He was seventeen years old with no license to drive, but he convinced his grandmother to sign her name on the title of a used sky-blue BMW 745, after he gave her $20,000 to purchase it from a used car lot.

A thick cloud of weed smoke streamed out of Kamil's mouth while he was seated on his grandmother's front porch, getting his hair braided by a hood-rat that lived down the street from him—

Devonaue, a low down, scandalous thirty-year-old woman with three kids by three different thugs. She made her earnings by braiding hair, scamming the government for checks or trading sexual favors for money from ballers who were horny idiots. Devonaue had just finished the last of the eight French braids in Kamil's head, then raised up from the porch with her hand extended, indicating to Kamil that she wanted her money. Kamil dug in his pocket and peeled her off a twenty-dollar bill from a small rubber banded stack of money.

"Get the fuck off my porch, cheap ass bitch."

"Since you wanna get smart, nigga, next time I'm charging your ass thirty dollars."

Kamil rose from the porch, laughing and watching Devonaue's big booty switch off in a short pair of cotton shorts that stopped at the bottom cuff of her ass. She looked at him and tossed up her middle finger. Kamil took out his car keys from his pocket and hit the alarm button to his BMW745. He climbed inside, checking out his braids in the rear view mirror that hung from the ceiling of the gray interior. He was a pitch-black, smooth-skinned youngster with small beady eyes like a snake and a pointy nose connected to his chiseled cheekbones. Before he backed that glossy-painted luxury vehicle off the dead grass of his grandmother's front lawn, a frail looking middle-aged woman came walking up to his car, knocking on the window.

Kamil rolled down the window. Looking at the woman, irritated, while she scratched her breast through the outer fabric of the white t-shirt she wore that read "Newport" across the front in green letters.

"Nephew, you got some work on you?"

"Damn, Auntie Ruby. Hold on, how much you trying to spend anyway? And don't come with no change."

"Little nigga, I got a crispy fifty, so let Auntie get a deal and get three grams."

Kamil leaned his body to the left and dug his right hand inside the back of his boxers. He pulled out a small tied-up plastic bag filled with rock cocaine and dropped one in the palm of his auntie's hand. She looked around for any signs of narcs or police cars then tossed the rocks in her mouth and walked off.

As a young boy growing up in a broken home on the Eastside of South Central Los Angeles, Kamil, aka K-Gutter, wanted more than anything the very things that it seemed he could never have—money, freedom, and power. He knew that if he didn't make it to the NBA, he was going full-time selling dope along with any other street-way he could survive, which was thieving and thugging. His mother was a crack-fiend who left his grandmother to raise him with two of his cousins and his father was a neighborhood wino who worked on troubled vehicles for small change, but was well skilled in his work.

Kamil drove off, heading to Demetrius' house on the Westside of Los Angeles, looking out for police while loving the smell and feel of the leather interior of his BMW—even though he was seventeen. He had the heart of a grown gangster and the strength of many grown men. Just like the rest of his close friends, his education came from the streets and his own rough experiences in an environment where he had to fend for himself. Before Kamil made it to Demetrius' house, he stopped by the carwash on 3rd Avenue and Vernon Boulevard. He made a left turn off Vernon Boulevard inside the carwash where several Mexican immigrants were washing cars. A carwash employee waved his hand in a gesture that was ordering Kamil to pull his BMW under one of the empty canopy spaces. Kamil got out of his Beamer and took a seat in one of the plastic white chairs against the office of the carwash. Watching his car getting washed and playing around on his touch screen cell phone, he made a call to Demetrius' cell phone to let him know that he was in the area by his house. Demetrius didn't respond to the call so Kamil left a text message. Kamil looked up from his cell phone and watched a Chevy Tahoe SUV pull in the canopy next to his BMW. He tried to look through the black tinted windows to see how many heads were inside, but it was hard to tell. He was waiting for the driver to exit, but they just sat there for a minute. When Kamil's car was done getting washed, a small fat Mexican with curly hair and a dirty t-shirt waved Kamil's car keys in the air. By the time Kamil rose from the chair, three guys exited the Chevy Tahoe, looking his way. Kamil watched the driver get out the driver's side, sporting a thick gold necklace around his neck with a medallion made up of a fist gripping hundred dollar bills engraved in diamonds. The guy wearing the necklace kept matching Kamil's glances every time Kamil looked his way until he flashed a gang sign at Kamil as Kamil shut the door of his Beamer and backed away.

CHAPTER 5

Montreal

Montreal, The third accomplice of the Nix's Check Cashing robbery, was the wisest of them all. He had no doubt that he was able to make it to the NBA coming from an environment in which he never expected to live past the age of twenty-five if he tossed his NBA dreams out of the window. The only reason he went on the robbery with Demetrius and Kamil was to prove that he had true thugness in his bloodline just like them, but he knew in his heart that it was a foolish stunt to pull and jeopardized his future goals. Montreal never touched his share of the money since the robbery and he continued to go to school and attend all his basketball practices and games while keeping a low profile, praying that not one mistake was made at the time of the robbery to lead the police his way and arrest him.

It was Westchester High School's last basketball game of the season before prom and they were playing Crenshaw High for the championship, blowing them away by seventeen points in the last quarter. Fresh out the hospital, Demetrius was well enough to participate in the game, so he promised Coach Pete that he would be there.

Scrilla was seated in the bleachers up top between two women who worked at his strip club, drinking on a soda through a straw, watching Demetrius alley-oop a dunk from Montreal's pass to him, barely missing the rim before the dunk. Demetrius hung on the rim after he dunked the ball, swinging his dick over the top of the head of one of Crenshaw's players and then fell down. They got in each other's face about to fight as everybody in the bleachers clapped and cheered loudly. The referee broke the two apart and the game continued.

Kamil was mad because he was sitting on the bench for showing up late to the game. During half-time he tried to make up a lie to Coach Pete that he was late because he had to work a job late, but Coach Pete was tired of his lies and his marijuana habits before the game. Before the end of the fourth quarter, Kamil rose up from his chair, kicked it over yelling, "Fuck you" to Coach Pete, and left the game.

After the game was over, Westchester students seated in the bleachers ran down off the bleachers to the basketball floor, cheering and celebrating with the team players. Scrilla got up from his seat with the two women, fixing his pistol on his waist to make sure it wouldn't fall. Halfway down the bleachers, he felt someone's hand tug on the shoulder of his black leather coat. He turned around and it was Demetrius' mother standing next to his sister Dominique.

"Hey, Vickie, before you begin to assume me of being the reason your son got hurt, it wasn't like that, and I've always tried to give him positive advice."

"Yeah, I know, Scrilla…I mean, Sean. He used to always tell me how you would run him off when he would try to come buy weed from you long ago and would give him rides to school and practices."

"You know you got my support, Vickie, whenever you need me."

Looking at the scar on his cheek from the bullet wound, Vickie made Scrilla step aside to talk to him out of her daughter's earshot.

"Sean, I know my boy is grown now and I don't know which lifestyle he will be wise enough to choose because he's at a confused state, but please don't tell him of my past with you."

"I can do that, Vickie. You still lookin good."

"Please don't go there, Sean."

In the past, Vickie helped Scrilla smuggle cocaine out of state a few times when she was jobless and a single parent; enough times to make ends meet until she found a job, then met Charles. Scrilla made a few passes at her, but she kept it strictly business!

Coach Pete walked up to Demetrius as he and his girlfriend, Amber, were hugged up and tongue kissing. He tapped Meech on the shoulder.

"Back in the locker room, I need to talk to you. Hi, Amber."

"Hey, Coach Pete."

Amber had been Demetrius' girlfriend since the ninth grade. She resembled Stacey Dash, but with a thicker figure. She was going off to college soon and wanted to spend her last days in Los Angeles with Demetrius until she left.

Back in the locker room where the team continued to celebrate, Coach Pete told everyone to quiet down. He grabbed a piece of paper from his clipboard and called out individuals who were recently offered a scholarship to a university. Demetrius was last to be called on the four-named list after he called Montreal to USC.

"Demetrius Williams…Stafford University."

"You bullshitting, Coach!"

"No, I'm not, but you got to get the rest of your credits straightened out this summer first and don't fuck up on probation."

While Coach Pete was giving his speech of celebration, Montreal and another team player snuck up behind him with a Gatorade plastic barrel and dumped the sports liquid all over him, leaving it to fall on top of his small, gray and black natural. He closed his eyes, yelling, "Practice is tomorrow, muthafuckas, and I don't give a fuck if it's the weekend!"

***

Kamil was in the parking lot by the baseball field, leaning up against the BMW with a small bottle of Remy Martin in his right hand, talking to a female while he recorded her phone number on his cell in the other hand.

Scrilla walked out the gym with his two female friends, looking at Kamil's BMW and its twenty-four-inch rims. He saw the car around recently and wondered which hustler was behind the wheel. The big booty, high-yellow female walked away from Kamil while Scrilla was walking up on him, smiling. They slapped hands and hugged one another then broke apart, smiling and facing each other. Scrilla was looking Kamil up and down from his shoes to the Dolce & Gabbana clear lens specks that covered his eyes with a black frame to match his black button up short sleeve shirt that had Dolce & Gabbana scribbled across the front in white cursive lettering. Scrilla was still smiling.

"Nigga, who you done robbed?"

"You know I gots to have my milk and cereal, big homie."

"What happened to your basketball career, you gave up on me?"

Kamil expressed a sign of regret and then looked down in shame, starring at his all black $500 Retro Jordan suede sneakers. "You know how it is, Scrilla. Mom's on dope, I ain't got no financial support and my big brother been in prison the last ten years. He was my last guidance before he left."

"This Beamer you?"

"Yeah, I just paid twenty stacks for it used."

"So what you gonna do with your life, young homie? Become an enemy to the public or strive hard and bring something back positive to the hood we all can fall back on?"

"I'ma keep it real, Scrilla. I'm cool on this school shit and basketball. Put me on, cuz, I want in and I'm down for whatever!"

"I ain't got time for mistakes, but come to my strip joint tonight. We throwing a party there for young Meech and Treal. They got offered scholarships to universities, so come support your homies. It's all on me."

Scrilla walked off with the two dime pieces that worked at his strip club and jumped in the backseat of a black Mercedes Benz 500 with tinted windows and drove away. Kamil drunk the rest of the Remy out the bottle and tossed it over the gate onto the baseball field. He jumped inside his BMW, turning the beat up on the stereo system and drove off making it his last time to be on school campus, and out into the world of "MOBBIN"—the career he wanted to master and become a product of. He was a young nigga in a wild life, criminal mind of a juvenile still living a child's life, being rushed to be his own man.

The marijuana dispensary on Crenshaw Boulevard was about to close in ten minutes to 9:00 PM. It was owned by Rick Rock, a local well-known drug trafficker in Los Angeles, trying to use the shop as a disguise, but his close homies knew that he sold pounds of weed for a reasonable price and rumored to be pushing the pounds straight out of his shop.

Kamil decided to get his belly filled with Jamaican Jerk Chicken before he hit the strip club and party. After he left Westchester High School, he stopped by Judy's Jerk Chicken on Crenshaw Boulevard to grab a plate to clean real quick. He was seated at a table that faced the glass window, showing Crenshaw Boulevard and Rick Rock's weed shop across the street. He saw a customer leave the shop and looked at his Cartier watch, realizing that Rick Rock was about to close. Kamil sucked the sauce from the chicken off his fingers, dug in his pocket and dropped a twenty dollar bill by his plate and got up to leave. He waved good-bye to the Jamaican woman behind the counter and fast walked out. He was trying to catch the shop across the street before it closed to get some blunts and weed.

Inside his shop, Rick Rock heard the doorbells while he was sweeping the floor toward the back door.

"We're closed for the night."

As he was turning around to face the customer, a chrome 380 automatic pistol was staring at him with a black masked face behind it.

"Go through the back door, nigga, and don't try shit, fool!"

"All the money is in the register, dog."

The masked man ran up behind Rick Rock's five-foot-nine, one-hundred-fifty-pound frame, and gripped the back of his white t-shirt, shoving him through the back door, and made him lay face down. He checked Rick Rock's waist and snatched a 9-millimeter Beretta from his waistline then hauled off a football goalie kick to his ribs. Rick Rock moaned in pain.

"Where them pounds and the safe at, cuz, because, if I have to search around and find it after you done lied to me, then cancel Christmas for this year?"

"I got six pounds in a gym bag in the utility closet and eighty-five hundred dollars in my bag with the pounds. Just don't shoot, dog."

He kept his pistol aimed at Rick Rock while he walked backwards about eight feet and opened the door to the utility closet. He saw the gym bag laying on the floor unzipped, showing off the plastic wrapped pounds and the stacks of money beside it, along with a sandwich bag full of ecstasy pills. He bent down and picked up the bag after closing the zipper, then walked up on Rick Rock.

Pop! Pop! Pop!

Three rounds crashed in the back of Rick Rock's skull, leaving blood flowing on the white floor. The masked man dashed out the front door and ran around to a back alley behind Crenshaw Boulevard, jumping in a sky-blue BMW and sped off down the pitched dark alley.

When he got to the end of the alley, Kamil rolled down his window and snatched the mask off his face. He reached his arm out the window, slung the black mask into the big blue dumpster and turned out the alley, blending in with traffic on Stocker Street. Turning on his music and bobbing his head to the beat, he slipped his Dolce & Gabbana glasses on his face.

***

Stella rolled her eyes at Scrilla and left to follow his orders. All eyes in the room were glued to the tattoo on her two ass cheeks that read "Thug" on the left cheek and "Bitch" on the right cheek in old English style red ink that matched her red curly hair that hung down to the middle of her spine. A lot of shit talking, boasting and bragging was going on at the same time the music was pumping loud through Scrilla's strip joint. Kamil was posted by Scrilla with a fat cigar in his mouth full of medical weed, at least eight grams stuffed inside the back wood cigar leaf. He whispered in Scrilla's ear then followed Scrilla out of the gambling room where they walked down the hallway past the strip area where more guys were posted around a five-by-eight stage, throwing money around a chocolate toned female. She was lying on her back naked with her long legs spread eagle, sticking the entire tip of a Moscato champagne bottle in-and-out her pink pussy lips, fucking herself while niggas were yelling and some against the wall in chairs getting lap dances by other strippers.

Kamil followed Scrilla to the end of the building until they went inside a small office and shut the door, locking it from behind. Scrilla took a seat behind his dark brown, shinny, wooden desk looking at Kamil take a seat in the chair in front of his desk with the cigar dangling between his black lips.

"So what you got to show to my interest, K-Hog?"

Kamil slid his cell phone across Scrilla's desk and took a drink from his Heineken bottle. Scrilla picked up the phone, analyzing the photo of three men at a carwash. Scrilla's face turned to anger when he saw one of the men on the picture wearing his gold necklace that got snatched from his neck the night he and Demetrius were shot on Crenshaw Boulevard.

"I want in, Scrilla. I know where them niggas hang at, and I'll make sure to send them to the Simpson Mortuary, cuz!"

"Once you in, it's Fa-Death-Doe, young nigga!"

CHAPTER 6

Demetrius stepped from the shadows inside an underground parking stall of a two-story apartment building in Hawthorne, California. He crept up to a dark blue, old model 1998 Lexus GS 400, and checked his surroundings before pulling a Slim Jim from the back of his Blue Dickie pants and stuck the sixteen-inch flat metal slab down the door through the bottom of the outside panel on the window. He moved it around for about sixty seconds then snatched it up and unlocked the door, tossing the Slim Jim on the passenger seat of the cream-colored leather. Demetrius began sweating at the forehead as he pulled a Phillips screwdriver and a pair of pliers from the front pouch of his blue hooded sweatshirt, clipped around the steering wheel column, breaking off chunks of plastic and then snatched down some wires, cutting away with the pliers. He connected three wires and the engine came alive with a noise-less humming sound.

Demetrius snatched the gate opener clipped to the sun visor and pressed the middle button. The gate began to swing open, he took his foot off the brake, and drove past a line of parked cars, dipping up out of the private garage. He left the city of Hawthorne on the 105 Freeway going eastward to pick up Kamil from his grandmother's house. Even though the Lexus was an old model, the car still looked new. Demetrius said a prayer to God while he drove on the freeway, because he finally made a decision that he would get his sixty credits this summer at school so he could graduate and put his scholarship to use and head for the NBA the next four years.

CHAPTER 7

Kamil was sitting down on his grandmother's couch, loading ammunition in a fifty round extended clip. He wore a pair of brown, cotton work gloves, being careful not to get any fingerprints on the bullets or the gun. He slapped the clip inside a mini-mac machine gun then sarcastically looked at Montreal, nodding and smiling.

"What you know about choppers, boy? You good in slam dunking that basketball, but let me see if you know how to slam dunk a nigga."

Kamil broke into laughter. Quietly seated across the living room in a single sofa chair, Montreal was looking nervous with a Heckler and Koch on his black jean covered lap. Fifteen minutes later, Kamil received a text on his phone and then he and Montreal left out the front door and jumped in the Lexus out in front where Demetrius was parked waiting.

The sun was setting, leaving the sky a dull orange color. Demetrius drove around Baldwin Village's entire perimeter looking for the SUV of the guys who shot him and Scrilla. After Kamil broadcasted their photos around on his phone to a few ruthless street cats, he knew he was given instructions to where they hung out.

The tenseness of such dark moments hit when Kamil was looking out the window of the passenger seat and spotted D-Dog, the guy who was first to run up on Scrilla's Chrysler 300M, brandishing his pistol then fired shots in the car. Kamil was hyped. He told Demetrius to slow down. D-Dog was leaned up against the front wall of an apartment complex, hugging on some woman, talking to her while a few more females and guys were loitering, drinking and smoking.

Demetrius sped up to the front then slowed down with three doors swinging open on the Lexus. Before D-Dog could run after he saw three masked men running toward him, holding pistols, everybody began yelling and ducking, and running. Bullets ripped through the back of D-Dog's bright red San Francisco 49ers football jersey, flattening him on his yellowish face, his hat flying off and one shoe missing. Kamil was holding the mini-mac with both hands spitting rapid continuous firing at everyone. He knocked D-Dog out of his white Nikes. The big tool had Kamil's wrist bouncing around because the gun was kicking hard in his hands. Demetrius ran up on three guys dressed in hip-hop gang attire and emptied the seventeen shot clip of his

P-89 Ruger. A few people got away, but most felt bullets that were a threat to them never physically returning to the world. The female that D-Dog was hugging caught a bullet close range to the front of her face when she fell on the grass looking up at Montreal's glock-40, pleading for her life, but he knocked her lights out like a cold-blooded gangster and this was his first body. He'd never killed anyone before, neither did Demetrius, but grimy ass Kamil had turned his two high school friends into killers. Pulling mob moves like grown, illegal living men.

The shooting popped off for a good two long minutes until the smoke cleared on the crime scene in front of the apartment building before the Lexus' back tires squealed off and left.

CHAPTER 8

Scrilla was always focusing on his paper as a gangster mack with at least a dozen women working at his strip joint and some pulling off financial capers on the sideline for him when they weren't sliding down the pole. He was once a famous dope boy in town, but he had to switch his game up when the Feds were riding his tail and did a "42-Fake" on their most aggressive squad, shutting down his dope house and renting out a building on the Westside of town, naming it Wet-Pearl's. He graduated from the super thug of survival because he'd come close once in his past when he beat an attempted murder case on one of his cocaine connects he robbed without no remorse. The supplier ended up dead before Scrilla's trail a year ago when he was subpoenaed to testify that Scrilla shot him in the back, therefore he was acquitted of all charges.

Drakes R&B album pumped through the inside of Scrilla's bachelorette condo-flat home located off Pacific Coast Highway in a suburban town called Palisades that had a cluster of million-dollar homes on a huge mountain overlooking the Santa Monica beach waters. Scrilla had over a hundred thousand in cash laid across his bed on top of some dark brown silk blankets, letting the bills run through his fingers like a money counting machine. He was shifting the currency through his palms so fast. He was lying on his side shirtless with a new necklace around his neck. His dark skin made the platinum piece shine even more from when he had his gold necklace that he gave to Kamil. Kamil snatched it off of D-Dog's neck after knocking his soul out of his body with the mini-mac.

Scrilla got up from the bed and began collecting the money, sliding it inside of a brown Gucci backpack, closing it up and tossing it in the closet. He walked out the bedroom as the music became louder, opening the door and taking a view of the living room. His jaw dropped when he saw Stella getting fucked in her anus with Diamond's tongue, in doggy-style position. The entire length of Diamond's tongue was going in-and-out like a small link snake. She gripped both of Stella's tattooed ass cheeks and rammed her face against it, tongue fucking her. Scrilla looked on with admiration in his black eyes as Stella's ass jiggled like Jell-O. He loved the sight of a redbone and a chocolate complexioned female going at it sexually. Diamond looked at Scrilla with her cat- shaped eyes and signaled him to join in, moving her index finger.

Scrilla strolled across the living room carpet in white socks, walking up to diamond. She unbuckled his Louis Vuitton "LV" belt buckle and pulled his black and red Monkey designer jeans down to his ankles with his boxers and grabbed his thick black penis, stuffing it in her mouth, sucking it slow until it magically grew long. Stella joined in and Scrilla gripped both of their hairdos while they both licked and sucked on his big black dick like some sexual animals in competition. Scrilla's butt muscles tightened up, oral sex was so good. He pumped his dick in and out of Diamond's mouth, fucking her face until he took his dick out and squirted thick amounts of cum out of his dick while Diamond and Stella's tongue were hanging out their mouths like two female dogs, licking and sucking his balls until he hardened again. Laying down on the thin black carpet, Stella climbed on top of him, grabbed his dick and guided it inside her pussy with one hand and bounced up and down on his dick. Her big, fat, plumped, dark nipple breasts were bouncing on every stroke. She grabbed her left breast and pleased herself by sucking it while she moved her hips in a circular motion, switching the gears on the stick. Diamond had her chocolate, wet, rounded black ass on Scrilla's whole face while he tongue kissed her pussy and licked her asshole. Both women were moaning loudly and kissing one another. Scrilla was popping his hips upward, gripping Stella's waist, thrashing his dick in her wet pussy hole like a fast rocket launcher.

CHAPTER 9

Demetrius was sitting inside the Monte Carlo Luxury Sport, warming up the engine about to go and sell it to a buyer. He promised his mom that he would go to summer school and embrace his scholarship as a gift from God. He backed out the garage into the middle of the street. Out of nowhere, undercover agents surrounded the Monte Carlo and drew their weapons on Demetrius, ordering him to stick his hands out the window. By the time Vickie made it out the house to witness the takedown of her son by authorities, the helicopter was hovering over their block and the agents had Demetrius on his knees, handcuffing him. The police blocked Vickie away when she tried to run up on her son. He looked at her through the backseat window of the black and white squad car as he rode away to get booked at the police station and charged for a 211 Robbery.

Kamil saw what was going on from two blocks away and drove off in his BMW, being thankful that he didn't arrive at Demetrius' house thirty minutes earlier when he was supposed to be there to pick him up, because he would have been part of the raid. As soon as the police took Demetrius and took his fingerprints in their 77 Division Station, he was marched in the Sergeant's office for questioning. From there on, he knew his scholarship was over and basketball career.

After he sat in the station for over three hours, Demetrius was sent to the County Jail and could not bail out because of the probation hold he had hanging over his head. He was sent to a six-man cell and given some blue LA County Jail pants and shirt to wear and met the five criminals in his cell that was charged with crimes, from burglary to murders. He called his mom collect on the pay phone inside the cell and a tear fell from his eye when he heard Vickie, his own mother deny his collect call.

***

Kamil drove to Montreal's house that was ten minutes from where Demetrius lived and saw Montreal being marched out the house handcuffed and wearing boxer shorts by four LAPD officers. Kamil looked Montreal dead in the face as he cruised by in his Beamer feeling nervous. Montreal put his head down like he felt shame. Kamil's conscience told him that the police was coming for him next. He called his grandmother's house phone, but no one answered. He drove to the trap house that Scrilla was letting him live in, packed his clothes and counted all the money he made from the last few days that Scrilla let him sell bags of weed out of the single bedroom. He called Scrilla from the trap house and informed him of what he witnessed at Demetrius and Montreal's house. Scrilla warned him not to go home and to stay low key, just in case the police had a warrant out for his arrest. Scrilla told Kamil to give up both of their full government names so that he can call the LA County jail and see what they were charged for. Meanwhile, Kamil was already feeling like a fugitive being forced into hiding. His birthday was the next day and he would legally be an adult—a fresh, eighteen-year-old, living life in the fast lane.

Kamil kicked up his Louis Vuitton Air Force One Nike's on the living room table and fired up a fat blunt of marijuana, thinking about his next move while a cloud of smoke floated around his face. A knock sounded off at the front door. He grabbed his tech-nine millimeter off the table and answered the door with the automatic in his hand, looking out the window like Malcolm X. A female was standing at the door, dressed in high heels and a tight pair of jeans hugging her legs and a small halter top.

"What's up? Who you looking for?"

"I'm trying to buy some weed."

Kamil let the female in and realized that it was one of Scrilla's female employees from the strip club. Kamil had a small mountain of Hydro—light green marijuana buds—stacked on top of the kitchen counter next to a digital scale. He started a conversation with the stripper and convinced her to kick it with him at the spot for the night. By midnight, Kamil had the thick, mean, good-looking female pulling down her Fendi Jeans and fucking him on the couch in the spot.

After Scrilla talked to Kamil on his cell phone while he was leaving his condo in Pacific Palisades, he got off the 10 Freeway going east. He exited the freeway ramp on Crenshaw Boulevard and ventured through a few hoods and blocks where the fellow hustlers were all fighting over the same limited number of corners and they'd stab you in the back in an instant.

Scrilla bent the corner on 63rd and Crenshaw, driving in his black Mercedes Benz on black rims. He was on his way to check on his spot that he let Kamil post up in the last few days. He saw a dice game popping off on the corner ahead and swerved his Benz up on the curb, parking on the side of the hustler's circle where they were crowded around each other gambling.

Scrilla yelled out, "What they hit Foe," gaining every one's attention as he pulled out a wad of bills from the pocket of his True Religion jeans and began placing bets, waiting for his turn on the dice.

Scrilla was well respected in the minds of the local thugs, but he knew some of the hustlers would stab you in the back in an instant, and some would try to take what you had. Scrilla, wearing a brown suede LA cap turned to the back, bent over scuffing his brand new brown Louis Vuitton Timberland boots, sitting on his knees with the dice shaking in the palms of his hands. A few eyes were glued to his thick, long, platinum necklace that had a diamond encrusted AK-47 machine gun attached to it. Several thugs at the dice game were sporting jewelry and holding cash in their hands to drop down on the sidewalk, but Scrilla had all eyes on him and he felt it when he heard someone from behind approach him.

"Scrilla, let me hold five hundred so I can try to win my money back!"

Scrilla turned around to look at an older hustler from back in the day he used to work for. The two-hundred-eighty-pound guy had the image of a football player, wearing a black Raiders football jersey and long French braids. He had his fist balled up, looking angry and mad because he lost all of his money.

"I ain't got no money to lend out to a nigga for 'em to gamble off. Shit, I can gamble my own shit off."

Tone, the guy that was begging Scrilla for money, got angry and swung his fist to the back of Scrilla's head, knocking him to the side. Tone was about to run up on Scrilla, who was now on the ground, but froze in his tracks when Scrilla snatched a .45-caliber from his waistband and pointed the chrome at Tone's stomach.

Tone tossed up his hands, smiling. "You got me, Dog. My bad, Scrilla."

"Yeah, nigga, your bad." Scrilla pulled the trigger several times, shooting Tone in his stomach. He waved his .45-caliber at the crowd of hustlers, causing them to disperse. Scrilla felt disrespected on his block that he had respect for and emptied out his clip on a couple of new faces that were running away from the dice game, dropping a couple of hustlers. He jumped in his Mercedes Benz and spun off. He looked in the rearview mirror at the swollen eye Tone had given him, wondering how he could possibly continue to succeed amid the chaos that approached him, and avoid all of the inevitable dangers he faced on the streets.

***

Later that day, after the chaotic shooting at the dice game, Kamil drove through the block in a tinted window, black Lincoln MKS SUV, jumping out and spraying rounds with his tech-nine. He wanted to send out a message on the block and show Scrilla his loyalty he had for him. Kamil left town, jumping on the 405

Freeway, headed to the bay area where his cousin lived, so he can lay low. Scrilla called him an hour later, giving love on the block and told Kamil that he was boarding a plane to Jamaica the next morning and to keep his phone on.

CHAPTER 10

A preliminary hearing was being held early morning on Demetrius and Montreal's first court day at the Los Angeles Criminal Court building. They had been locked in the Los Angeles County jail for two weeks. Scrilla made it to the Caribbean, chilling with his family in Trench Town, Jamaica. Kamil was laying low in Oakland, California, keeping in touch with Scrilla from the cell phone. They were thinking like fugitives, traveling with cash to survive.

Vickie was up early in the morning, sitting at the kitchen table sipping on a mug of coffee looking stressed. She was getting ready for Demetrius' court day, so she was forced to take off work. She grabbed her carton of cigarettes from the table and her car keys, walked out the front door, and climbed inside of her 4-door Lexus SUV with her purse slung over her shoulder. She backed out the driveway and as she drove down the block, she slowed down and stopped in front of the corner house, rolling down her passenger window to the lady down the block who was watering her front lawn.

"Good morning, Ms. Francis."

The elderly woman looked up and smiled shyly at Vickie. She sat down her water hose and walked out of her front gate up to the passenger's side of the Lexus truck.

"Hi, Vickie, good morning to you too."

"If you still need a job, Ms. Francis, I can get you hired at the County building where it's less dangerous."

"Oh sweetheart, thank you, but after that robbery at my old job, Nix's, I think I need a break."

Vickie waved Ms. Francis good-bye and was on her way to the court building.

When Vickie made it to the courthouse, it took her at least thirty minutes to find a parking space. She felt bad for not accepting any of Demetrius' collect calls for the last couple of weeks he'd been in jail, but she felt betrayed after finding out the crime he was charged with after he made a promise to her to gain his high school diploma for the summer and graduate.

Two hours later inside of the court room where Vickie was seated watching young black men get sentenced off to prison with terms long enough to leave them with gray hair or possibly die in prison for the crimes they committed. Vickie said a prayer for her son, that the huge white judge would be a bit easy on him. Vickie was seated in the front row, looking at the woman district attorney verbally abuse a young teen who was charged with felony assault. After the frail, white blonde rested her case, the judge found the young man guilty without any physical evidence or eyewitness to take the stand, and sentenced him off to state prison for eighteen years for his time in jail as an adult.

The young, black man charged at the district attorney and socked her in the mouth, breaking her jaw before he was tackled and beaten from behind by three Bailiff Sheriffs. They dragged the young thug out of court, telling him to "Shut the fuck up!" He was yelling out gang profanity and making threats to kill the judge.

Demetrius' case was next. Ten minutes later, the Bailiff escorted Demetrius and Montreal into the courtroom to be seated in front of the judge. As Demetrius was being led out in shackles, he looked around for any family support and spotted Vickie dressed in a long sleeve white dress with her hair pressed down, wearing a gold necklace and earrings. Vickie still looked beautiful at the age of forty-two, but you could tell that she had been stressing by the bags under her eyes and the worried looks.

The judge looked at Demetrius and Montreal and banged his wooden gavel on his podium to get the court's attention. He held a white piece of paper, looking through his glasses and speaking in the microphone.

"On June 23, 2005, defendants Montreal Davis and Demetrius Williams were arrested on robbery case G-67389. In that case, three masked men dressed in black allegedly to have committed an armed robbery inside of a Nix's Check Cashing business and held three employees hostage. An extra charge of kidnapping will be added to their case and I'm going to raise both of their bails to a million dollars each until the next court day."

Demetrius' public defender, a small Hispanic man, informed him that his probation hold was uplifted and the best thing to do on their next court day was to file a motion for a bail reduction. They were escorted out of the courtroom and Vickie talked to the public defender for about thirty minutes before leaving the courtroom. She was informed that Demetrius had an informant on his case and his co-defendant, Montreal, was about to have his case separated from Demetrius'. Vickie collected a copy of the police report and walked out of the courtroom with Mr. Hernandez, Demetrius' lawyer.

CHAPTER 11

Kamil drove across the Bay Bridge feeling a bit nervous and smoking on a Newport cigarette. While he was on the freeway, his cousin, Sharon, called him on his cell phone and told him that detectives showed up at their grandmother Rita's house looking for him to ask a few questions.

Running on his last three thousand dollars, money was becoming important for Kamil. , He left his BMW parked in the backyard of his grandmother's house and convinced the hood rat, Devonaue, to rent the Lincoln MKS under a fake I.D. and bogus credit cards and he promised to look out for her after she gave him the keys to the rental, before he shot up 63rd Street, going to the bay afterwards.

Kamil arrived in the bay area at 4:00 AM. The sky was still dark. He still had a lot of energy from the ecstasy pills he popped the night before with the stripper he was laid up with all night. He left her in Scrilla's spot asleep and never told her that he was leaving.

Kamil had a .4- Caliber machine gun on the passenger's seat. He'd taken the gun from Scrilla's spot just in case he ran into any danger in the Bay where he had no one but his cousin, Armond, he hadn't seen in a couple of years.

As Kamil drove down a main street that was unknown to him, he kept trying to call Armond for the directions to his house in Vallejo, California, but there was no answer. He left messages to let him know that he was in town. Kamil was about to break himself into the Bay on some gangster shit as he looked at the time on his Jacob watch, driving past a Wells Fargo Bank.

He reached in the backseat and grabbed a Louis Vuitton gym bag he had his clothes in and dumped all of his clothes out onto the backseat. He made a U-turn in the middle of the street. He received a text on his Droid cell phone and saw his cousin's address on the screen and a message telling Kamil to call him. Kamil laid low on a side street for another hour, smoking cigarettes back-to-back.

When the time hit 6:00 AM, he drove back up the main boulevard and swooped the Lincoln MKS up in front of the bank, jumping out, hugging the monstrous .45-caliber machine gun and the brown Louis Vuitton duffel bag. His black LA baseball cap was sagging low over his eyebrows matching the black bandana tied around his mouth cowboy style, only showing his eyes.

It was still early and only four clerks were working at their tellers with one old, baldheaded, skinny security guard who was walking around looking too relaxed. Kamil exploded through the double glass doors, brandishing the army style machine gun, cursing.

"Get the fuck down, everybody! Kiss the fuckin floor!"

The old security guard dropped his cup of coffee and tried to pull on the .38 special in his holster, but was knocked down by a few .45-caliber hallow-point slugs. Kamil's black Michael Jordan sneakers squeaked across the glossy hardwood floor as he leaped over the counter and snatched a woman clerk from the floor, gripping her blonde hair, talking an inch close to her face.

"You got ten seconds, bitch, to fill up this bag, hurry up!"

The young pretty blonde-haired woman ran back-and-forth to at least four cashier windows, filling up the Louis Vuitton bag with brand new bills. Kamil ran up on her, snatching the bag from her hand, and made her lay back on the floor before he dashed out the bank into the SUV and fled away.

CHAPTER 12

Demetrius was cocked back on his bunk inside of a cell at the Twin Towers facility that was part of LA County men's central jail. He was reading a book called *Destruction of Black Boys* that he borrowed from his cellmate's personal library on the top shelf. Four months had passed away since he'd been incarcerated. He still was under a lot of stress even though he had stopped dwelling on his failure to go to college and play professional ball. The main issue that would create anger inside of him while being locked away was that he still hadn't received any mail or money orders from his close friends or family. His girlfriend, Amber, could only do so much for him, working a minimum wage job inside of the Fox Hills Mall for Hot Dog on a Stick. Other than Amber's support, his mother Vickie would drop off a hundred dollars on his Inmate Trust Account every two weeks so that he could have food to eat and toiletries to wash his body with every day.

A voice on a loud intercom echoed through the small square speakers that were built on the white painted brick walls inside of each cell, and names for visitation were called out. Demetrius sat the book down to listen for his name, and his was called. He got up from the bottom bunk and walked to the sink, and looked in the mirror. Brushing his small fade that was turning into a small natural, he smoothed lotion on his face and walked out the cell past the Day Room, greeting all the thuggish inmates who were either sitting at a four-seat small steel table playing poker, or exercising against the back wall doing pull-ups up under the stairs.

Demetrius walked down the visiting row past a few inmates that were seated behind the Plexiglas window, talking to their visitors on the other side. Demetrius was expecting Amber or his mother, Vickie, to be at the window waiting, because the both of them took turns every weekend visiting him on Saturdays and Sundays or they would travel together with his little sister Dominique.

When Demetrius made it to his assigned seat and window, a strikingly beautiful African-American woman was seated, and a wide warming smile formed on her face when she looked at Demetrius with her golden brown eyes that matched her golden brown shiny smooth skin. She had long blondish-brown dread locks that were neatly twisted and cut at the ends. Demetrius was still gazing into her eyes as if she had him hypnotized. It took him at least a long five seconds to pick up the phone and he finally spoke.

"Hi, whoever you are."

The black queen giggled at Demetrius' greeting, then she sparked up the conversation after clearing her throat, a serious expression covering her pretty glowing face.

"First and foremost, Mr. Williams, I am your new attorney that was replaced by Mr. Hernandez, your public defender. Are you familiar with a male figure, thirty-three years old with the name of Samajay Combs aka Scrilla?

"Yeah! Why?"

"There's no need to worry, Demetrius. The reason why I asked is because he paid me fifty grand to represent you on your case."

Demetrius' soul glowed at the mentioning of Scrilla showing him major support and keeping it real to the game like real homies should. He really had the conception that his comrades left him for dead and was beginning to say fuck Scrilla and Kamil.

"He gave me a message and told me to tell you not to worry, and just keep it real and no matter how desperate the police get by offering false deals, don't fall victim."

"What's your name, Miss?"

"Oh, I'm sorry, my name is Khadijah Salaam. You can call me, Ms. Salaam or Khadijah."

"I like Khadijah. Plus it's an attribute of God in Islam.

"How'd you know that, Mr. Williams?"

"I'm not just a street thug, I mean, I do study and had dreams to go to the NBA."

"Yeah, I know your whole story by talking to Samajay and having conversations with your mother."

"So what's going on with my case?"

Khadijah pulled some legal court documents from her black briefcase and slid her Coach glasses on her face.

"Mr. Williams, the way things are looking right now, as far as the evidence they have on you, you're facing twenty-five years to life, plus ten years for the gun enhancement and fifteen years for kidnapping, which makes the worst equal at least fifty years. The good thing is that you have no adult criminal record other than the criminal charges you caught as a juvenile."

"So since Scrilla paid you, what kind of relief I get?"

"With my successful skills throughout the criminal court field, I can at least get you a deal for ten years after getting the gun charge and kidnapping dropped, plus I went to law school with your District Attorney. But, we have two problems to work on—your co-defendant Montreal Brown agreed to the police at the station when you two first got locked up to testify that he never knew you were robbing the Nix's and lied, saying he was just catching a lift to basketball practice from you and some unknown person with the moniker of K-Hog.

"And what's the second problem?"

"A lady name Ms. Francis, who was working at the time of the armed robbery is supposed to testify that your voice is the voice she heard giving orders and she recognizes, but she's scared to show up, I believe."

"So, what now?"

"Well, the DA knows that Montreal is a liar because his tattoo on his right forearm of the "L-A" initial was caught on security camera, but if you give up the third person, aka K-Hog, you can get less than five years."

"I'm not opening my mouth, Khadijah, so just do what you got to do for me. I'm ready to face what I half to."

"Well, you go to court in two months and I will file the final motions for a plea deal due to lack of evidence, but I will half to go to trial if our motion gets denied. I have a strong feeling that I can cross up both witnesses in examination and shut them down. Don't worry, pray to God!"

Khadijah blew Demetrius a kiss, got out the seat, and disappeared from the window. Demetrius' feelings were torn down after receiving documents with Montreal's statement typed in black and white ink. He got angry and had visions of killing Montreal, blowing his brains out on to the floor. Montreal's street credit was no longer valid. He had turned to a stool pigeon within twenty-four hours of being interrogated and tricked at 77-Division Police Station. He had a time limit to go into protective custody, because word got around quickly inside of ruthless ass Los Angeles County Jail. Demetrius immediately requested a pass to the law library the next day by his dormitory officer and got multiple copies made of Montreal's state sheet.

CHAPTER 13

Scrilla swaggered through the Trench Town, a small village in Jamaica, dressed in black baggy jeans, a black Fedora hat and black Timberland boots with a white t-shirt, smoking blunt after blunt as he viewed around at the poorness of the country, a place that slave traders used to take slaves back in the early 1800s. He was homesick and was eager to get back to the U.S. He was just waiting for the phone call that he was supposed to receive from his family lawyer, Khadijah, the young woman he hired to fight Demetrius' case.

After Scrilla shot Tone in the stomach at the dice game, Scrilla was thinking ahead just in case Tone or anyone else was snitching on him. He would already be out of the country before the U.S. would shut down his travelling visa and passport. He could have gone back to his hometown, Shreveport, Louisiana, to lay low with family members, but he chose Jamaica, where lots of his mom's side of the family resided and plus, he had business with his Uncle Desi to sit down and talk about before he left Jamaica. Meanwhile, he was staying with his Aunt Judi in a small hut with at least five children under the same roof.

The small narrow dirt road that Scrilla was walking down was cluttered with raggedy looking sheds that were made for homes the Jamaican people were living in. On the side of each home was a long piece of string tied to trees or sticks coming up from the dirt that was made for hanging clothes to dry. All the villagers hanging out waved to Scrilla or said, "Hi," as he passed by their houses. The day was turning to night and fireflies was flying around in packs magically lighting up the community where half the places had no electricity. Scrilla saw a group of Rastafarians hanging out in front of a lighted shed, smoking marijuana through long waded pipes and playing Jamaican tunes through an instrument called a Rumba Box—a square wooden box with strings of metal. A couple of Jamaican women had Banjos, shaking them and matching the beat that the old Rastafarians were playing on the Rhumba Box. Scrilla walked up to the counter top in front of the shed and started speaking in the Jamaican language, ordering a twelve pack of ginger ale Jamaican brew and a pound of Jamaican Jerk Chicken. The old Rastafarian who was sitting on a Pepsi Cola crate smiled at Scrilla with a mouth void of teeth when he noticed Scrilla staring at the Jamaican woman's large ass moving, who was shaking the Banjos. The woman's ass was so big and firm, it looked like she had two butts growing into one that was twice the size of the model Buffy's ass. Scrilla asked the man behind the wooden counter where he could buy some Ganja, the phrase they normally used around Jamaica for marijuana. The guy pointed at the toothless Rhumba Box player and yelled a few Jamaican words at him. The toothless man stopped playing the Rhumbo Box, took off his cotton, colored, tall hat from his dreadlocks, and pulled out three ounces of weed in three separate plastic bags. He held up ten fingers and said, "American Dollars," to Scrilla. Scrilla pulled out a hundred dollar bill, handed it to him, took all three ounces, grabbed his groceries from the counter and walked off up the road. The Rastafarians waved good-bye to him until he was out of their sight.

Trench Town, Jamaica was struggling with a chronically stagnant economy and had one of the highest crime rates in the world. Even though Scrilla's Jamaican Uncle Desi was a well-respected mafia boss around Jamaica, Scrilla wasn't foolish enough to sport his jewelry around grimy areas like the one he was currently living in with his Aunt Judy. While he was almost home, he looked over his shoulders as an old Jeep drove past him up the road with three Rastafarian thugs inside looking at Scrilla as they drove by him. When they were gone, Scrilla pulled out his cell phone and called Uncle Desi.

***

Ms. Francis sat in her bathtub, scrubbing around the top fat layers of her breast and then squinted through her glasses at her surroundings, looking for her towel to wrap around her nakedness. She stood up in the tub, dried off, grabbed her bathrobe that was hanging on a hook plastered on the wall by the sink and mirror and then she climbed out the tub. She faced the mirror, fixing the glasses on her face then she bent over picking up her stockings from the top of the toilet seat and began rolling them up to her thighs. As soon as she lifted up her full body, a large figure stepped inside of the bathroom behind her and wrapped his muscular arms around Mr. Francis' neck, covering her mouth with a leather-gloved hand before she could even scream for help. In the mirror, she looked into the man's eyes while he stood behind her before his right hand gripped the back of her neck and rammed her face into the mirror with full force, knocking her dentures out her mouth and onto the bathroom floor. He rammed her face repeatedly until the mirror cracked into pieces, leaving her face with thick, dripping clots of blood.

The man wearing the black mask with eyeholes dropped Ms. Francis' body to the floor and kicked her in the ribs a few hard times before bending over her and checking her pulse. Then he left her home after stealing all of her jewelry from her bedroom.

CHAPTER 14

Kamil was drowning his troubles in a bottle of Hennessey hoping that he didn't have a warrant out for his arrest for the Nix's Check Cashing robbery after receiving word on the LA Streets that his boy, Montreal, was snitching on the case. Meanwhile, he was still residing up North in Oakland, California, holding onto a lot of money and ready to relocate once he got a call from Scrilla. He was chilling with his cousin Armond inside of his dope house, in the middle of the night, watching dope fiends come in and out the spot with stolen merchandise to trade for coke. As Kamil's phone started to ring, he picked it up from his lap while laid back on a small sofa in front of a small glass table with Ziploc bags filled with coke and wrinkled currency inside of a blunt box.

"Hello, who is this?"

"This Montreal, my nigga, what's good?"

"How you get my number?"

"Your grandmother gave it to me after she accepted my collect call. I need your help, Dog."

"What's up?'

"The judge just dropped my bail. I'm about to bail out, but I don't know who I can trust, because this nigga Meech speaking bad on me, telling niggas I'm a snitch. I think the nigga is mad because I'm about to bail out, hating and shit."

"So what you want me to do?"

"I need you to clear my name up for me and help me relocate. I still got money stashed away."

"Fuck what niggas saying, you gonna always be my true homie. Just call me when you bail out, because I'm not in town. But I got to go."

Kamil hung up the phone and called Scrilla's cell phone.

"Scrilla, what up, fool? You still in Jamaica?"

"Yeah, but I'll be back real soon, on some other type of hustle that will have my pockets fat like Beyoncé's thighs, little nigga!"

"That punk ass nigga, Treal, just called my phone pleading his case, saying he ain't snitching and he about to bail out and he needs me to take him to get his stash and clear his name on the streets."

"Man, that nigga lying, K-Hog. Meech's lawyer mailed me a copy of all the paperwork. He didn't tell on you so just play it cool with him for the meanwhile, because he trusts you. The police just looking for me for questioning about my name being implicated in the shooting on 63rd Street, but my lawyer said I'm not more than a person of interest, so I'm all good."

"I'm leaving Oakland tonight then and I'll call you when I get back to LA."

"Meech's trial starts in two weeks. He might have to take a deal for ten years and do eight out of that, but I'll holler at you soon and call me as soon as you make it back down south. By the way, I thought the police raided your grandmother's house on the eastside?"

"I found out that the motherfuckers wasn't never the police, they was some niggas playing like the police and tricked their way past my grandmother through the front door and stole eighty-three hundred out my room."

"You know who did it?"

"Nope, but I'll find out. I'm sitting on eighty thousand in cash right now and I just purchased me a new whip. That eighty-three hundred didn't hurt me."

CHAPTER 15

The detectives had just left 63rd Street visiting Vickie and her husband, Charles, questioning them about Ms. Francis' murder and if they saw anybody visiting her house the day she was murdered. Vickie felt sorry for the single living senior woman, but Ms. Francis was a threat to Demetrius catching a life sentence. Just for the kidnapping charge alone, if she were to testify at trial. The murder of Ms. Francis was recorded at the 77 Division Police Station as a home invasion robbery murder due to all of her jewelry that were dumped out of the box.

Vickie was standing over the kitchen counter chopping up onions and celery trying to prepare a meal, which she hadn't done in a while, and relieve some stress from within. Amber stepped beside her.

"You need some help, Ms. Williams?"

"No, honey, I can handle it. You need to be resting anyway."

Amber walked out the kitchen rubbing her small protruding belly. She was eight months pregnant with Demetrius' baby.

She had a debate with her parents, arguing with them constantly, telling them she wasn't getting an abortion and no longer cared about going to college at the present moment, so they kicked her out the house and she was currently staying with Vickie, sleeping in Demetrius' bedroom.

"Smells good in here, beautiful."

Vickie turned her head to the deep voice and Charles walked up on her in front of the stove, planting a kiss on her mouth and looking her in the eyes.

"Baby you need a break. I'm taking you on vacation right after you go to Meech's sentencing date."

"And how are you going to do that when you just got laid off?"

Charles pulled out a fat wad of money from the black slacks he was wearing and flashed it at Vickie.

"I won thirty thousand dollars on my lottery ticket I purchased last week."

"Oh Charles, baby, where we going?"

"Wherever you want to go."

"Africa."

"Then that's where we going and Amber is too. She needs a vacation from that boy of yours leaving her knocked up like that. I paid the mortgage and all the bills for the next two months."

Vickie grabbed Charles and wrapped her arms around him, hugging him tightly. He pulled away when he heard Amber calling him, yelling out to him that Demetrius was on the phone and wanted to talk to him. Vickie followed him in the living room and saw a bunch of shopping bags with baby boy clothes Charles purchased for Amber's baby.

"What's up stepson? How you doing?"

"I's straight Charles, did you find that?"

"Yeah, thanks."

"Nah, thank you, but we gonna stop here."

"You know what's up, baby boy! But me and your mom's and sis along with Amber will be at your court day next week. Then, I'm taking everyone to Africa."

"Damn, I wish I could come."

"You'll be home soon. Keep ya head up like Tupac says. Here's ya mother."

Charles handed the phone to Vickie and went outside to the backyard to look at his low-rider he had purchased after Demetrius gave him his share of the Nix's Check Cashing robbery to kill Ms. Francis. Charles still had some thug life trapped up in him from his past, even though he was now a family man. But, he would always be remembered on the streets as a notorious Eastside Crip gang commander from 118th Street, East Coast Block Crips.

Charles had kneeled down on one knee drinking an Olde English 800 beer in the backyard starring at his candy-coated painted, Raspberry Blue 1992 Cadillac Fleetwood, four-door Low Rider with switches and sitting on one hundred-spoke, triple good Daytona wire wheels, having memories of his public enemy days.

CHAPTER 16

Montreal was lying on his top bunk inside the six-man cell, fighting the urge, trying not to tell the county jail Sheriff Deputies to check him in the protective custody module. He was in a cell full of ruthless, heartless thugs that were questioning his street credit daily, because of his funny ways, and was wondering why he didn't possess any of his paperwork for the crime he claimed that he was in jail for, which was murder. A boldfaced lie that he told the Blood Gang members when he entered their cell. He was trying to sleep away the day, waiting to get bailed out of jail. His bail was dropped to one hundred thousand after he promised to testify against Demetrius for a lesser sentence. Montreal hadn't eaten any food the jail was serving, except for the sack lunches and the dessert off the dinner tray. He felt like he was living in hell and every day was like a test to his manhood.

He woke up from the long nap when he heard his last name being called.

"Williams, come sign for your canteen."

Montreal climbed down from the bunk and walked to the front of the cell, sticking his hands through the steel gate and signing the receipt to his hundred dollar bag of food his mother put on his books for him to purchase for the week. The canteen Mexican lady dressed in black uniform slacks and a gray collar short-sleeved shirt pushed his bag through the tray slot and left. The entire cell was looking at the bag of food like vultures.

"You ain't gonna offer none of the homies no food, Blood?"

Montreal dug in his bag, pulled out five Snickers candy bars, and passed one to the brown skin thug with French braids who was talking to him from the back bottom bunk against the wall by the pay phone. Then he dished the rest out to his homies in the cell. Montreal looked bewildered and tried to place the bag on his top bunk above the thug's bunk who wore the braids, but he reached for Montreal's bag.

"Give me this, Blood."

"Ain't no way in hell you takin' mine!"

Montreal tried to defend his property and manhood, but he was getting packed out by all five thugs in the cell. They were beating him so badly until he yelled for the deputies to save him. One of the guys decided to search through his green property bag, found some paperwork, and begin to read through it. After they jumped on Montreal, they made him lay on his bunk after tying his mouth up with torn sheets. Thirty minutes later, the young thug who was reading the paperwork, with tattoos on his face, blurted out loud in the cell, "This nigga's a snitch, Dog!"

They snatched Montreal from his top bunk and held him against the back wall of the cell. Montreal's eyes grew large when he saw one of them reach under the bunk and pull out two long ice picks and handed one to another one of their homeboys. Montreal tried to struggle out of the grip the three thugs had him in, but it was too late. He was being stabbed in the face and neck. At least twenty punctures covered his body the next morning when the deputies found him stuffed in the laundry cart inside the day room.

A week later, the entire cell was charged with Montreal's murder due to Montreal's name being logged in the books as being housed in their cell.

After his last court date, Demetrius took a deal for ten years and he was sentenced to prison for better or worse.

CHAPTER 17

A lot of hustler's from different street organizations never understood how Scrilla was getting paid after he left the dope game alone and several were jealous because each one always failed when trying to set Scrilla up for a robbery plot, but everyone wondered how he had so many women on his team. Those who knew him personally, except for his close female companions or family who were trustworthy, knew where he lived and laid his head. They only knew about the small apartment on 63rd Street where he hung from time to time, but rarely saw him there.

Scrilla changed his cell phone number and cut contact with Kamil after hearing about him robbing the bank up north in the Bay area, because he didn't need any unnecessary attention. Besides, he had a feeling that Kamil was young and reckless and could easily attract the Feds to him. So, he planned on catching up with Kamil later and let him enjoy the streets. While he was on vacation handling business, Scrilla shut down his strip club and was working on building a new improved one in two different states once he got his money right.

Scrilla's Jamaican uncle, Desi, had sent someone to pick up Scrilla from Aunt Judy's hut in Trench Town, to bring him back to his home in Kingston, Jamaica, to finish business before Scrilla was to fly back to the USA. He sat on a milk crate in front of Aunt Judy's hut, drinking a ginger ale and smoking a joint of marijuana, waiting on his ride to Kingston, and watching the children in the village play around, enjoying the heat.

"I think that's my ride coming, Auntie."

Scrilla hugged Judy then grabbed his luggage from the ground as an emerald green Land Rover drove up in front of them and stopped. Two Jamaican law enforcers were seated in front wearing military looking uniforms with dark shades and hats to match their green camouflaged uniforms. The officer in the passenger seat of the truck looked at Scrilla's puzzled look on his face.

"We are sent by your Uncle Desi. Get in the backseat, my boy, and let's go before the storm comes in."

Scrilla opened the back door, tossing his luggage in first and jumped inside, closing the door. From the back window of the Land Rover, he waved at his baby cousin and aunt until it was gone from their side of the village.

Desi had an entourage of corrupted Jamaican officers working for his regime that were willing to break any law in Kingston to gain his loyalty. The government tried to overthrow him decades ago, but his alliance was too strong, and had powerful friends from different nations and a bit of European power backing him in his evil illegal doings.

Scrilla had fallen asleep in the backseat after smoking over four blunts with the soldiers who were driving him to his uncle's home. It was raining by the time they made it to Kingston, Jamaica. The bumpy road caused Scrilla to wake up when the truck rocked from side to side. The Jamaican who was driving pulled the Land Rover up to a big black steel gate and stuck his hand outside of the window with a small looking credit card between his index fingers, sliding the key inside a triangular hole of a podium with a keypad similar to that of a bank's ATM.

As they drove closer to the black-painted large imposing residence, Scrilla looked out the window through his Gucci shades at all the young soldiers walking around the compound clutching M-16 machine guns, wearing military uniforms. The young Jamaican soldiers looked to be no older than thirteen years old, maybe younger. Desi was known for scooping poor young boys out of poverty-stricken villages, taking them off their family's poor hands and training them to be his loyal killers and protectors like an inner-city street hustler trains a Pit Bull from the stage of a puppy. On the top roof of the black mansion hung a big yellow and green Jamaican flag with a few armed guards with walkie-talkies. Scrilla looked at his uncle's power with admiration as he climbed out of the backseat of the Land Rover with one of the soldiers helping him with his luggage to the front door.

The double black wooden doors swung open and Desi was standing in front of his nephew dressed in black Khaki pants, a thick brown leather blazer coat and dark brown Rockport dress shoes. His hairstyle was cut into a small level high top fade, exactly like the rapper Lil Boosie's hairstyle. He was clean-shaven, standing at six-foot-five.

Desi smiled widely, looking at Scrilla. "My nephew, show me love, my boy!"

Scrilla embraced Desi as they both entered the mansion. A soldier took Scrilla's luggage upstairs to a room while Desi introduced Scrilla to a few of his friends that were congregating in the large guest room, next to the living room as they came through the black glossy wooded door's with glass squares in the middle. There were a few European old and middle-aged looking men dressed in suits, standing around holding drinks inside of glass cups and a few wealthy looking black men. African paintings hung on the walls and African sculptures around the room, mostly of naked women. In the far back end of the guest room through two more wooden glass doors, Scrilla saw a group of young looking beautiful women, huddled around inside of a large hot tub dressed in swimsuits, laughing and playing. It was at least seven or eight model-looking women from different nationalities, but most from Jamaica. Scrilla made contact with a few of the beauties, they flirted with him by waving, and one flashed her bare perky breasts at him. Scrilla recognized one of the girls as one who was smuggled in America a couple of years ago to work at his strip club and escort service. Once she made enough money to support her family, Scrilla sent her back to Jamaica. Some of the women who worked for Scrilla's were fresh from overseas and different countries. The local women in the inner city who flocked around Scrilla for a job were more problems because he had to deal with a lot of jealousy from the inner city thugs and high-powered businessmen who were losing their relationships to Scrilla's dangerous mackin.

Stepping out of the circle of the different race of men that were entrepreneurs from all over the world mingling in Desi's large guest room, Desi gained everyone's attention, shouting.

"Gentleman, gentleman, let's begin our meeting. My nephew from the United States of America has arrived."

Everyone took a seat at a large long black shinny piano wooden table, while Desi was still standing, walking around the table, passing out Cuban cigars and taking orders for specific drinks that certain bosses wanted. He handed the slip to one of his soldiers standing in the room with an M-16 strapped over his shoulders and began with his speech while everyone got quiet.

"Gentlemen, I greet you all here on the bank of Kingston, Jamaica. First, I shall thank you all for networking with each other and sharing our women within each other's businesses within our nations where we reside for financial gain. Some of you gentlemen have asked about my nephew Sean, known as Scrilla, and his method of controlling his women because several of his women begged to be returned back to him after falling into the hands of some of you. So, here is the young man. Stand up, Nephew."

Scrilla rose from his chair, walked to the front of his uncle's guest room, and began speaking to the rich audience.

"It's a pleasure to be in the presence of power, which is all of you, especially for me, a man who started off as a petty corner drug peddler, robber, and graduated to drug trafficking and moved on. We are hated by the world and an enemy to the public of the world. I have experimented with lots of methods to control my women without threats and force. I look at it as a secret and a gift and that secret is that you have to make love to the minds of every last woman who works in your stable. Why? Because when you first receive them, they already look at themselves as worthless slaves and are torn by being away from family, if they had any that cared. If installed correctly, I guarantee you that you will control your women without a headache for at least a good three years or more; and some will want to stay with you forever.

"Number one, you must be a Mack to be a boss and you must make your women feel that you are worthy to be followed. Number two, the only fear you should instill in your women is sending them back to where they came from after they begin to love you and, never, never beat or abuse your women when they anger you, because that is a quick way for them to bring the law down on you and ruin everything you worked hard for in life. Even your legal earnings. A few teachings that can help you step your game up is age, intelligence, size, attitude, style of hair, respect, admiration. A lot of men in our field will try and constantly give their women drugs to control them or make them feel comfortable. You don't need to feed them drugs. That ruins your cattle. Teach them how to dress, how to eat the right foods, exercise, how to con tricks, and the main method and secret is, how to love you."

Everyone in the guest room began clapping, while some had taken out small notes pads to write down notes.

One small Italian guy dressed in a leather black Gucci suit and dark Gucci shades with his hair slicked back with a shine shouted, "No wonder why my girls wants to request to go to

America or always mentions this slick fucker's name, Scrilla. Scrilla, or I want Sean."

Everyone in the room began laughing loudly and drinking as the meeting ended.

Scrilla was involved in the cruel game of human trafficking, doing business with millionaire and billionaires who were well respected in their nations and some were even crooked politicians. After the meeting, Scrilla had several business offers from different bosses that wanted to invest in him or partner up with him in their country. He recorded several contacts and names in his iPhone. He knew he had several mornings and sleepless nights waiting. Hard work, dedication, creativity, execution and one man could never do it alone. He couldn't be solo anymore. He needed other men with loyalty, trust and intelligence on his team that he could do business with back in the city where he already had one of the most popular strip clubs in Los Angeles. However, when he returned he wanted to build one in New York and a bigger one in Los Angeles. Scrilla didn't plan to be in the trafficking game for long, because California was making a law with stiffer penalties for human traffickers. Scrilla just wanted young women who turned to the streets when they had nowhere else to go. But, he still had some morals left in him, because he didn't accept any women under the age of eighteen, although he was committing the second highest grossing criminal act. Desi was getting away with the crime for so long, because he had the majority of Jamaican police on payroll and the Jamaican police department has long been plagued by accusations of corruption and illegal killings.

Desi told Scrilla he was coming to the USA right behind him to buy a house and open a few businesses because he just found out the Jamaican police chief would soon get all new recruits and they will be required to take a lie detector test to ensure the department's integrity and professionalism. Even those working for Desi was due to take a polygraph test soon.

CHAPTER 18

10 Years Later

Demetrius was finishing up his last year of incarceration with little support. The last three years had taken a toll on him with a few tragedies. His son by Amber was now eight years old, going to elementary school and Amber gave up on him and left him for dead. His first few years in prison and the only time he received pictures of his son was when his mom sent them or they would take pictures in the visiting room when Vickie and Dominique would drive down to Corcoran State Prison to visit Demetrius.

Throughout his entire struggle, Demetrius grew stronger. Every dangerous prison incident he faced, he attacked with boldness from inmates owing him debts, neutral combat, fistfights, to bloody race wars, which turned him into a militant thug with three hundred sixty degrees of secret knowledge that he learned from several books. He was twenty-eight years old, going on twenty-nine upon his release, with a bigger and stronger body from exercising, with tattoos like a rap star.

"Yard recall, yard recall, everybody take it in and return all rec-yard equipment," said the prison guard in the tower overlooking the entire prison yard. He locked a bullet in the chamber of his rifle after he was finished calling an end to the yard over the loud microphone.

Demetrius was finishing up his last sets of pull-ups on the pull-up bars, grunting on his last rep before jumping down and flexing his muscles. He moved through the crowd of different race groups and gangs with his shirt off, wearing nothing but his state issued blue prison jeans and brown prison boots, wearing black leather gloves and his mean mug on his face; the look from black thug men that evoked fear, unsettled nerves and changed the atmosphere of virtually any room, and able to make a white person walk on the opposite side of the street in a single bound.

After Demetrius greeted a few of his close comrades and said his good-byes before he left the yard, he passed by a female correctional officer and she stopped him in his tracks before entering his housing unit.

"Mr. Williams, slow down and let me talk to you for a quick sec."

The full figured woman made sure no inmates were ear hustling and tilted her glasses over the tip of her nose before speaking.

"So, when will I see you again, because I'm aware that you're being released tomorrow and I know you not going to forget about me after I snuck all those cell phones in for you to make some money to get by?"

Demetrius made his chest muscles jump. Ms. Grant smiled and her pussy tingled for Demetrius with anticipation.

"Baby, I'm a fuck you hard when I catch up with you. Just let me get settled and I'll give you a call."

Demetrius walked inside his dormitory housing unit and locked himself inside his cell. He profited twenty grand from Ms. Grant bringing him cell phones—two a week—that Demetrius sold to inmates for $1,000 each. She flirted with him when she started working at Corcoran Prison a year ago and was sucking his dick from time to time in the back of the main kitchen where he worked, but it was never enough time for Ms. Grant to give him some pussy, because of the count time. He had to make it back to his cell, so that he wouldn't be reported missing. Ms. Grant was a thirty-five-year-old black woman with a short curly hairstyle, brownish color, and a big ass and huge breasts, causing inmates to flirt with her constantly while Demetrius never paid her any attention until the day she confronted him, grabbing on his dick, talking sexually.

When Demetrius got back inside his cell, he took a bird bath over the sink, dried off and dug inside of his locker, pulling a small cell phone from the inside of a oatmeal box wrapped in plastic. He unraveled the plastic, turning the phone on and checking his messages. Khadijah, his attorney, had left him two messages. Khadijah was a constant supporter of his struggle, sending him motivational books and greeting cards on every holiday and birthday, but never visited him, because she knew that her husband wouldn't understand their casual friendship.

Demetrius viewed the first text that read, *Last day in prison, hope you've learned your lesson.* The second text read, *You are invited to a dinner date of real food. Would you like to come?*

Demetrius slipped his Trey Songz CD inside his CD player and let it play through every song as he went in his stash and rolled him a joint of Kush weed, got high and then called Khadijah.

She answered on the first ring. "Hi, Demetrius."

"What's cracking, my black queen? It's good to hear about your offer to a dinner date, because I didn't think twice on that."

Khadijah giggled. "Demetrius, I really hope you get out here and get on the right track, because there are a lot of good black men trapped in prison and your son needs you."

"You know it's hard on a felon, Khadijah, but I can promise you that I'll try."

They both got quiet for a second, and then Demetrius started back up.

"So have you heard from Scrilla?"

"No and I don't want to hear from him ever Demetrius. He's a disgrace to every woman of every nation. I'll explain to you over our dinner date, okay? But, call me when you're free."

CHAPTER 19

A huge jet plane was parked in a hidden civilization off the coast of the Caribbean Sea. A group of women—mostly non-white—were standing side by side; a sort of different origins from Japanese to Brazilian, back to the Middle East. Desi and Scrilla were draft-picking, scouting through all the natural beauties that they would profit from whatever work they placed them in when they finally smuggled them all the way in the U.S. safely. All the women were naked, except for a small pair of underwear they wore. Daniel Rockford, a white male who was to fly the plane to the U.S., was checking the temperature inside of the plane. At the bottom, was a secret compartment was built out of special metal that was big enough to hold at least twenty-five women if they were laid down side by side like slaves on the ancient slave ships. It was designed to take in oxygen from the atmosphere to make it easier for the women to breathe from the bottom of the plane. The plane was shared by a group of crooked powerful men that pitched in on the twenty-million-dollar jet. It was equipped with a radar system like the police helicopters that was advanced enough to read street signs from three hundred feet above ground.

Daniel was ready to board the women. They filed in one single line and began walking up a small metal ramp. After the women were on the plane, Daniel closed the ramp after giving them instructions how to lie down. Desi handed a white male dressed in a suit a briefcase filled with money, then he and Scrilla boarded the plane with Daniel, ready to fly away from the secluded area surrounded by palm trees and huge bushes next to the sea.

Scrilla had become the highest paid street hustler in California ever since Demetrius' incarceration. Without a doubt, he was labeled a millionaire just by the new Maybach he drove around at various times that was witnessed by all the LA criminals and drug dealers. He had opened a luxury club in New York City and a new strip club in Hollywood, California, along with a couple of escort services in Las Vegas, Nevada, and a professional massage parlor that sold sex.

***

"Nassir, don't you dare talk back to me, boy! I told you to eat your vegetables first and then you can go and play that damn game!"

Amber glanced at the digital clock on the cooking stove, and then walked to her bedroom to start picking an outfit to wear to work. Her son, Nassir, looked identical to Demetrius, except he was a lighter shade with hazel brown eyes like his mother.

Nassir scraped his mixed vegetables off his plate into a napkin and balled it up. He got up from the table and tossed it inside the white plastic trashcan in the kitchen. He heard a thump and then another and twisted around looking at the window by the kitchen table and walked up to it. He smiled, ran and unlocked the front door!

Demetrius stepped inside, closing the door behind him and Nassir jumped in his father's arms, squeezing his neck tightly.

Amber heard a man's voice and yanked her bedroom door open. Walking back into the living room, she stopped in her tracks as if she'd seen a monster or ghost, covering her mouth in shock.

"Oh my God, Meech. I thought you had life in prison."

"Shit, if I did, you couldn't even stick around the first couple of years or bring my son to see me. I just told you that to see how strong your love is for me."

Demetrius put his son down and shoved Amber away when she tried to embrace him.

"You had years to do that when I was locked up for ten years, but I ain't trippin' on the past. Just get my son some clothes so I can take him with me for the week."

Amber smirked and released a few tears, feeling hurt and remorseful for at least not visiting or sending photos in the mail when Demetrius got to prison.

"Meech, you can at least give me credit for taking good care of our son and not just look at the negative. I'm sorry. Okay?"

"Yeah, you sorry alright. A sorry ass stripper! Nigga told me how you work for Scrilla all in his new strip joint, but you a grown ass woman, do you. Just go and get Nassir's clothes so I can get out of here."

Amber felt embarrassed and walked out the living room. It took her about thirty minutes before she returned to the living room, holding a black duffel bag filled with Nassir's clothes.

Demetrius was sitting on his knees play fighting with his son, and stood up when he heard Amber sitting the bag on the living room floor.

"Look Meech, I had lost my job and I just worked at this strip club for a year, just enough to save me some money until I got a job. I'm sorry."

"I ain't trippin, but I gotta go. I'll call you when I'm ready to bring him back."

Nassir gave his mother a hug and kiss, then he and his father walked out the door. When he got back to his mom's house, everybody was asleep. He played video games on X-Box with Nassir for a couple hours and talked about his school before putting him to sleep in his old room and he slept on the couch in the living room.

CHAPTER 20

The next morning Demetrius woke up at 5:45 AM. His body was still accustomed to waking up early every day in prison. He still had his clothes on except for his shoes when he lifted up from the couch and walked to the bathroom to take a shit. After using the toilet, Demetrius turned on the shower, peeling out of his white long sleeve thermo and blue jeans, leaving them on the floor. After he was done showering, his mom started banging on the door.

"Meech, you got fifteen minutes left in there. I gotta get ready for work."

"Okay, Mama, I'll be out in a sec."

Demetrius was still shitting out prison food, tried to spray some of Charles' cologne in the air to kill the smell then put the cologne back in the cabinet, and walked out the bathroom with a towel around his waist into the bedroom. Nassir was sound asleep in the bed while Demetrius was getting dress in the middle of the floor, as he looked at his son sleep. He felt he had to get himself together financially quick, without going back to prison. He returned to the streets virtually back to square one. The money he earned before he got locked away was all gone, and the money he made in prison by selling cell phone he owed to Khadijah for fighting an AD charge of Residential Burglary the LAPD tried to place on him while he was in prison and brought down to court for a couple of months.

Charles was sitting at the kitchen table eating bacon and grits, watching the news on the small kitchen television on the counter facing the table when Demetrius walked in.

"What's crackin', baby boy! Your mom made you a plate and put it in the microware before she left."

Demetrius gave Charles a handshake, and sat across the table from him after grabbing his plate from the microwave.

"So what's been going on in the neighborhood, Pops?"

"Shit, these niggas been knocking each other's heads off. They forgot the old school version, using your hands. At least after you get that out of the way then you all have respect for each other. But they got these guns in play and they been driving me and your mom crazy at night. We gotta move!"

"You still got your job at the construction company?"

"Fuck no. Meech, that white man ain't playing fair out here. You barely see a black face working on construction sites in the hood. Last time I showed up at work, me and a few brothas joined in on protesting and took it to the streets to demonstrate outrage over the lack of black men and women working on construction sites in Los Angeles."

Demetrius starred Charles in the eye, looking sincere before he spoke. "Say, O.G., I really respect and love how you proved your loyalty for me by knocking that old snitch bitch, Ms. Francis, off to save me from a life sentence."

"It's like this, Meech. I love your mom and I love you like a son, and I knew how your mom would have been broken down if that bitch testified in court on you and gave you a 'L.' Your mom don't know and don't need to know, but the felling is likewise, cuz."

"So what you doing today, Pops?"

"My low-rider car club is putting together a peace rally to promote peace between the Crips and Bloods. We will be low riding through most of South L.A. and end up at Imperial Beach later on, to Bar-B-Q and set some rules. You want to roll?"

"Yeah, let's roll. Let me go wake up Nassir and feed him something to eat."

"Well, I'm about to make a liquor store run and you and your bad ass son should be ready by the time I'm pulling up in front of the house."

By the time Charles pulled up in front of the house, Demetrius was sitting on the front porch with Nassir eating ice cream and enjoying the sunny weather. Nassir was the first to get up and run up the front sidewalk out the yard grabbing on the back door of Charles' 1992 Cadillac Fleetwood low-rider. Charles stuck his head out the window looking at Nassir holding the ice cream cone.

"Boy, you know you ain't eating in my ride, and go rinse off your hands so you won't get my leather sticky!"

After Charles drove away from the house, his first stop was to meet his car club at Leimert Park, located on Crenshaw Boulevard on the Westside of South Los Angeles. Charles slipped his oldies but goodies CD inside of the Alpine Stereo system and let The Drifters echo through the speakers inside the gray leather interior while they cruised up to the park where everyone was waiting. Nassir peered out the back window excitedly as he took in a good view of all the old school to new school low-rider cars lined up at Leimert Park. "Oohs and ahhs" fell from his mouth and he began tapping on Charles' shoulder from the backseat.

"Make it hop, Papa. Make it hop!"

Charles had an open can of beer between his legs as he pulled up to the front of the park. As he cruised past the red light, a can of Olde English 800 flew out the driver's side window. Charles' reached down under the dash board of the CD player, tapping on one of the eight switches, jacking the entire frame of the car up on four wheels then he made a right turn into the park with the right front end of the car lifting up on three wheels, wheeling into the park. He then dropped the car down, causing everyone's body to shake and bounce.

"Hell yeah, Papa. Do it again!"

Demetrius looked at Nassir in the backseat with wide serious looking eyes.

"Boy, you better watch your mouth; your little ass ain't grown."

Charles busted out into laughter as he found a parking space. "Yeah, you got a handful, Meech. But, one thing I can say is, his bad ass bring home good grades. You want a beer?"

"Hell nah, Olde English is played out, Big C. I'll leave that for you old niggas to drink."

They exited the car and Charles introduced his car club friends to Meech as his son and Nassir as his grandson. The park was packed with gangsters up in age and a handful of youngsters. Big Steve who used to work the construction site with Charles came through the park riding on a glossy cherry red Harley Davidson motorcycle with a chromed out engine. Pulling next to Charles low-rider, he jumped off his bike and gave Meech a hug.

"Damn you got big, boy. What the hell they was feeding you in prison?"

Demetrius laughed as Charles went inside the trunk of his low-rider, pulling out a fifth of Seagram's Gin and a bottle of Donald Duck orange juice with a bag of plastic cups. He passed out cups to his car club friends, pouring everyone a drink. Fat Mouse, a beady-eyed, six-foot-five old school dark skinned gangster from Compton with French braids grabbed the bottle of gin from Charles and gulped down the remaining of the liquor.

"Woo shit! This some strong shit, Charles. You got your strap on you, Big Homie?"

Charles dug in the inside of the trunk by one of the hydraulic batteries and pulled out a P-94 Ruger, flashing it to Fat Mouse. "Nigga, I stay with my bitch."

Demetrius cringed when he saw Charles pull the firearm from the trunk, because he knew Charles was a crazy alcoholic who would try to prove himself if he got drunk enough, plus he was on parole.

The Reputable Riders low-rider club cruised around Los Angeles city followed by a group of Harley Davidson motorcycles, passing out peace promotion flyers and showing off their rides to the on-lookers. When everybody finally carpooled to Imperial Beach, the crowd grew bigger. Imperial Beach was the place to hold gatherings. The sand was filled with vendors from all over the area; there were food and drink vendors like Jamba Juice and Dr. Pepper, BBQ, Shaved Ice and a stage for rappers to perform. While Charles was trying to find a parking spot on the street curb up the hill from the beach area, a car of young gang-bangers came racing up Pacific Coast Highway inside of a 1995 burgundy Impala on twenty-four-inch chrome rims with a royal-blue four-door 1986 Malibu Wagon on twenty-two-inch gold Dayton wire rims on the side of them, going full speed with a tailpipe that was barking like a gigantic bull dog. Five seconds later, a black and white police car hit the red and blue lights on the Dodge Charger unit, chasing after the gang members who were racing each other, tossing red and blue bandannas out the windows of their cars.

Charles and Fat Mouse walked down the hill drunk with Demetrius behind them holding Nassir's hand. When they got down on the sand, Fat Mouse walked up to a Bar-B-Q Grille, sagging in his blue Dickies, Chuck Taylors sneakers, demanding a plate of food from the female wearing a booty-cut skirt behind the grille.

"I want everything on the plate and at least six or seven ribs!"

The female on the side of the Grille snickered as they prepared plates of food behind a long table.

"Nigga, you can at least say please!"

"Gangsta's don't please nobody, bitch; you know that!"

"Fuck you, Mouse!"

Fat Mouse snatched up his plate and began to devour the food animal style. The DJ was mixing up between old school and new school while people danced on the sand by the large stage. Demetrius and Charles found some shade to drink under by a group of females and car club members. Nassir ran off with a few kids to beat on a Piñata in the shape of a car trying to bust out the candy.

After Demetrius got a bit of liquor in him, he loosened up a little, looking at all the ladies, while swigging on a cold bottle of Moët Champagne. A high yellow female with two other women strutted by Demetrius. She was wearing a short jean skirt with a pair of white Channel sandals and a white leaf shirt with a long ponytail and dark shades on her face. Demetrius reached out and grabber her hand, squeezing it lightly. She tried to yank away until she noticed who grabbed her hand.

"Hey Meech, nigga I ain't seen you since high school. You look good, boy! When you get out of jail?"

"It ain't even been a week, Pinky."

Demetrius let her hand go and saved her number in his phone.

"Nigga you better call me tonight. I'm trying to get that dick while its fresh."

Pinky was a good friend of Amber's and knew how she left him for dead in prison, but she also knew that Demetrius was a go-getter for his money and looks didn't really matter, because she was known for messing around with Crips and Bloods who were hood rich. She hugged Meech and kissed him on the cheek before she walked off.

"What you lookin at, old man?'

"Girl, I'll fuck the shit out of your young ass!"

Nassir heard Charles' rude flirtatious remark at Pinky and sounded off loud. "I'm telling Granny on you, Papa."

"Please don't, boy! I won't bring you with me no more." Charles dug in his pocket and gave Nassir a ten-dollar bill. "Now you better not say anything to your Granny, and I told you if you snitchin', you can't hang with the men!"

"Okay, Papa."

Nassir ran off with the kids, and Demetrius and Charles continued to enjoy the shade and converse with the car club riders. Demetrius paused and looked up the hill at a 2013 white Cadillac Escalade SUV, sitting on white and chrome thirty-inch rims. The truck parked and three guys piled out, tugging on their waist looking around as they moved through the crowd. When they came closer by the Bar-B-Q Grille, Demetrius saw a familiar face. He watched them approach the same group of women that Pinky was with then he recognized the face up under the yellow and purple Lakers basketball cap with braids hanging out the sides talking to Pinky's home girl, Keisha—a five-foot-ten dark fudge color female with a gorgeous smile and long micro braids with a tiny waistline and big butt. When Kamil got closer by the canopy Demetrius was posting under, he threw up both of his hands.

"K-Hog, what up my nigga?"

Kamil heard his name being yelled out and saw whom it was and cracked a wide grin, walking up on Demetrius giving him a hug. While Demetrius was gone for ten years, Kamil became one of the savviest hustlers in Los Angeles, twisting niggas left and right. He embraced Charles also and said, "What's up?" to the rest of the old gangsters standing around.

"Man, we got to catch up, Meech. What you doing tonight?"

"Just chilling; going back home to Mom's house and get my son ready for school."

Kamil went in his pocket, peeled a couple of grand from a small roll of cash and gave Demetrius all C-notes.

"So when you want me to slide through?"

"I'll be up in the morning, so I'll hit you when I take Nassir to school."

Kamil spent the rest of the day at the beach with Demetrius catching up a little on who got killed, who got locked up, and who was balling out of control, and what new beefs were transpiring between different gangs. The peace promotion was shutting down early because a group of different Crips and Bloods gang sects started a brawl in the middle of the beach. Demetrius had to run and grab Nassir and they left.

As Charles was starting up his car waiting for Demetrius and Nassir to close their doors before pulling off, multiple shots rang out. The Cadillac Fleetwood made an electrical noise, the entire body frame of the car jerked up in the air, and Charles skirted off from the beach looking at everybody run around wildly through the rearview mirror, placing his P-94 Ruger on his lap. Charles was drunk and angry.

"Punk ass young niggas always fucking a good time up! What if my grandson or any other kids would have got shot?"

Charles' eyes were blood shot. When he pulled up to a red light going eastward up Rosecrans Boulevard, the burgundy 1995 stock Impala pulled up on the left side of Charles' Fleetwood. The young thugs were mean mugging him, making him nervous as he kept catching eye contact with the passenger that sported a red Phillies baseball cap.

Demetrius felt the tension growing.

"Don't pay those clowns any attention, Pops."

Charles cocked the chamber back on his pistol, grabbing the handle.

"Lay down, Nassir. Lay down now!"

The guy sitting in the passenger's side flashed a gang sign at Charles and his door flew open. Charles quickly stuck his P-94

Ruger out the window, squeezing the trigger until he couldn't pop off any more shell casings and knocked the amateur thug back against the Impala with a few rounds ripping through his chest cavity and ricocheting through the interior of the Impala. Charles smashed his foot on the gas pedal until it was touching the floor, turning off Rosecrans onto the 110 Freeway.

"Papa, I want my mamma."

"Don't worry, baby boy, we safe. Just don't tell no one, okay?"

"I'm no snitch."

Demetrius grabbed his son from the backseat and made him sit between him and Charles. He was a tall eight year old.

CHAPTER 21

"There is no nation on Earth that has less
respect for and as little control of their woman
as we so-called Negroes here in America. Even
animals and beasts, the fowls in the air have
more love and respect for their females then the
so-called Negroes of America"
— The most honorable Elijah Mohammad.

Scrilla came through the door of his main office at Wet Pearl, his new rebuilt strip club in Hollywood, California and plopped down on his brown leather chair behind his desk. He then loosened his tie, took off his gray silk jacket from his Armani suit, and laid it across the back of the chair he was sitting in and began counting some money on the top of a brown shiny wood grain desk. When his count of the currency flipping through the palms of his hands reached three grand, a small nock on the door bumped a couple of times.

"Yeah, what up?"

"Prophet, can I go home early today? My stomach hurts."

"How much money did you make in tips tonight already?"

"Altogether, eighteen hundred, and five hundred of that came along from this white man who continuously wanted lap dances."

"Did you dance good on him, baby?"

"I think I must have, because he came on himself."

Scrilla chuckled and kissed the young beauty's neck. She was nineteen going on twenty, a former housemaid slave from the West Indies who was proud enough to eat at McDonald's. Naomi grabbed Scrilla's dick like a vice and began moving her grip around in a circular motion.

"Um, nice size, Prophet. I think I love this."

Scrilla's dick grew large and hard as a stone. He became curious and reached in his top desk drawer, grabbing a Magnum rubber, because he slipped up a few times and raw-dicked a couple of his top notch women, especially the virgin foreign young beauties who were smuggled from overseas after getting tested for HIV.

Naomi snatched off Scrilla's necktie and tossed it on the floor. Pulling Scrilla's dick from his Armani slacks, Naomi fingered the head of his disk, giving him a hand job. She stopped right before he came and then climbed on top of his lap sliding her thong to the side to fit his dick in her slippery pussy. He grabbed her hips and ripped off her gold top sucking her breast wildly. She finally let him come while he was still licking and sucking her small perky breasts.

"I love you, Prophet. Don't lick too much because milk will be in them soon."

Scrilla didn't respond for a brief second then made her climb off his lap. Zipping his pants up with the condom still rolled on his dick, he became serious.

"What you mean, milk?"

"I'm pregnant with your baby."

"You gotta get rid of it. You gettin' an abortion!"

"I don't need you to help me take care of it, I'll do the rest!"

Scrilla pulled a mini 40-glock from under his desk and pointed it at Naomi's stomach. "I'll shoot you in the stomach or I can send you back to Jamaica. Which one, bitch?"

Naomi sucked her teeth and became teary eyed. Scrilla made her leave the office and left out behind her. When he was leaving out the door, Dudley was just about to escort another female to his office door. Scrilla looked away from the door lock and saw who it was and told Dudley to take Naomi home and he would be fine.

Amber stood in the hallway rummaging through her purse then took out a pair of keys and handed them to Scrilla.

"Here's my keys to my locker in the dressing room. I quit, Scrilla. I found me a job to support my son. Thank you."

Before Amber tried to walk away, Scrilla grabbed her arm.

"Let me go nigga! I ain't one of these immigrant ass hoes who slave for you."

"Didn't you read the Business Agreement to this club when you signed up for the job? Didn't you? I got a copy in the office and you still owe me a year's worth of stripping. I ain't no suck ass corner pimp making chump change. I'm a business man!"

"Nigga, you don't own me!"

"Bitch, I tried to look out for you when you came crying, 'I'm Broke,' after Meech went to jail and plugged you in with tricks that was papered up enough to put you in that Lexus. I need's mine!"

Amber was angry and filled with mixed emotions.

"Nigga, do not disrespect me as a black woman."

"You faggot ass broke bitch, you better give me another year, or you can give me fifty grand, or I'm having Dudley take you to Small Claims Court."

Amber hauled off and tried to kick him in the dick, missing and kicked his leg. Scrilla punched her in the eye after she tried to rush after him and knocked her smooth out like a thug on the corner. She hit the ground hard, grabbing her swollen eye. Stella saw the whole thing walking around the corner of the hallway with Desi.

"Scrilla, what happened?"

"Stella, ya girl out of line. She attacked me first. It's all on video camera." Scrilla pointed to the small camera in the corner ceiling of the hallway, grinning and looking at Amber.

"Now you assaulted me first, so be a dummy and call the police if you want, because you going to jail if they see the camera."

Stella kneeled down over Amber's body, checking her face. "Are you okay? Let me take you someplace and get you fixed up."

Scrilla seemed like he wanted to kick Stella in the face until she looked up and winked her eye at him, indicating that she was bluffing.

Desi and Stella helped her up and she began to gain a little of her inner self and awareness and started cursing at Scrilla loudly.

"Nigga, I'm a get you killed, I swear!"

"Get her out of here now, Desi. Take her out back and dump her in the alley!"

The back fire escape door of the strip club swung open and Desi had his arm gripped around Amber's neck and let her go.

"Leave, Amber, leave now!"

Amber looked in Desi's eyes, saw a warning sign and turned around to walk away. When she twisted her head, she heard a thin piece of metal click. Scrilla came from behind Desi through the door and tried to shoot her in the back of the head. She took off running after witnessing her life flash when she faced the barrel of the glock.

"Damn!"

Scrilla tried to hurry up and cock a bullet in the chamber and squeezed off a few rounds, barely missing Amber as she dashed behind a trash bin, hollering, and then took off running again until she got out the alley at the corner and ran to her car in front of the club, still screaming.

CHAPTER 22

"How about a drink, Meech?"

"That will be cool, because I need one right now."

"I'll take a glass of Vodka mixed with cranberry."

Demetrius had just arrived at Khadija's office after Vickie rented him a 2012 Buick Regal G.S. for a couple of weeks to handle his business and look for employment.

Khadijah made sure her office would make her clients feel like home when they visit. It had a small kitchen area and a mini bar inside the office space.

Khadijah came back in the office area holding a glass of Vodka in one hand and a small bottle of Welch's cranberry juice and placed it down on the small glass coffee table sitting in front of Demetrius while he was cocked back on a small fluffy burgundy suede sofa.

"Thank you, Khadijah. You a sweetheart."

Demetrius dug in his pocket and pulled out a neatly stack of bills and sat it on the coffee table.

"That's the twenty grand I owe you for knocking off that Residential Burglary case for me while I was in the Pen."

Khadijah hesitated and then grabbed the money from the table.

"Meech, I don't know quite how to put this, but it's funny, because for some strange reason, I don't feel right taking my own money."

Khadijah laughed and walked back in the kitchen. Demetrius studied her backside and watched the two healthy looking firm butt cheeks wiggle through her business slacks as she disappeared through the kitchen door. Wrapping her golden brown dread-locks into a ponytail, she began to Google a food recipe from her laptop on the counter by the stove to prepare some Chicken and Shrimp Fettuccini Alfredo with Lobster Tail. She was definitely a dime piece without a doubt at the ripe age of forty-five. Preserving her beauty by eating healthy and staying clean from drugs as her days when she was young going to high school and college. Demetrius' phone kept going off and he kept rejecting calls from his baby mamma, Amber. While he was sipping on his Vodka, looking at Khadija's graduation plaques on the walls of her office—dedicated work of honor at Howard University Law School—she was giving Demetrius a strong urge to get his weight up financially, because Khadijah was the type of woman a street nigga would cup-cake around with while using hood rats for nothing more than a sexual pleasure or busting a quick nut at a horny moment.

Demetrius smelled the aroma of a valuable meal in the air tickling his nostrils and walked in on Khadijah while she was standing over the stove cooking and talking on the phone at the same time.

"Yes, Scrilla. I mean, Sean. I can no longer be connected to you, nor represent you on any more charges and God bless you don't get into any more trouble. Sean, I don't care how much money you offer me, don't take it personally, but I can't deal with anyone involved in that filthy business you have going on. Now that's it! I'm cleaning all of your money you paid me to be ready on your side and empty it out of my bank account first thing in the morning, because I already took half out this morning."

Scrilla hung up in her face, angry because she didn't want to be his personal attorney anymore after beating cases for him and his hustling friends for years.

"This food is almost done, Meech. Do you like lobster?"

"Of course, boo, I'm a mobster."

"Oh my God, Meech, you are a mess." Khadijah giggled at his jokingly sense of humor and began preparing the food on two black plates, bringing them to the table and sitting them down gently before taking a seat across from Demetrius.

"Oh, that was your friend, Sean. I'm not dealing with him, Meech, anymore; and, I promise you that if I find out you're involved with what he's doing that will mess with our friendship badly."

"What the nigga got going on?"

"You don't know yet?"

"No, Khadijah, we ain't hooked up since I been at home or talked."

"He's involved in a huge human trafficking ring, smuggling teenagers and young women from mostly third world poor countries and the Caribbean where I met him fifteen years ago."

"What the hell he doing that for?"

"You never wondered where all the beautiful women came from that's been working for him since you've known him? They start at eighteen years old, but that's no excuse for manipulating women for financial needs!"

"Damn, Khadijah, that's some crazy shit, because I would see shit like that on the news and in newspapers I read in prison. I'm no angel, but I still got morals within me that's strong enough to not let me go down that road."

"I'm not trying to break up you guys' friendship, because he did a good deed by hiring me to represent you for the robbery case, but I'm done on that subject."

"So, how's your divorce going?"

"Oh my God, Meech, he's a mess. Some people just don't learn how to let go. He's constantly acting like a pest. He cheated on me twice after giving him eight years of dedicated love, but to answer your question, I'm at peace because it will be over between us soon at our last court day coming up."

After they were done eating and spending a little quality time discussing life, Meech got up and extended his hand, but Khadijah rejected the shake and hugged him, then kissed him on the cheek good-bye.

Amber was sitting inside of her Lexus trying to hold back her tears, looking in her rearview mirror at her swollen black eye. She couldn't fight it no more and slammed her fist on the steering wheel. It was a particularly dangerous life for a female hustler, and Amber was feeling that she had to build an intimidating presence to protect herself from now on after Stella falsely played her into trying to aid Scrilla to end her life. Her only soft spot was her son after she got the picture that Demetrius was not trying to fuck with her anymore.

Demetrius called Amber back as soon as Khadijah closed the door behind him. Before he left from the top cemented steps of her office, he waited for a moment then peeked through her front window and saw Khadijah dumping a purse-sized bag of freshly wrapped money on the coffee table, and then she revealed about four more bags with money.

CHAPTER 23

Kamil was up early in the morning bagging up drugs at Devonaue's home. A Section-8 two bedroom that was up to code, but you would have thought it wasn't from the way she kept shit lying over the place. Dirty dishes were always in the sink, the floor was always caked with grime and several of his sister's kids, along with hers, ran in and out the house all through the day light hours with the smaller ones of the bunch flocking behind them begging any grown-up in the house for ice cream truck money.

Kamil served two years for Residential Burglary within the middle of Demetrius ten years. Upon his release, he earned an average amount of reasonable cash from a murder contract he signed off on for Scrilla and never saw his other half of money owned to him so he continued to burglarize homes, rob other thugs and punk the street game at his best, as usual. The only redeeming he formed in his two-year stint at Folsom State Prison was he became smarter in his scandalous deeds and fiend more for currency. He was, in fact, a wicked and cruel person and loved his friends who ascertained the same traits as him.

Kamil did not intend to sell dope upon release. But, needless to say, the Mexican holiday—Cinco De Mayo—was not too far from behind, and that plundered a cocaine drought in his hood on the eastside. The Mexican Mafia was still short on dope and he planned on dumping a few zones out of Devonaue's house while he had the manipulation tactics to do it, knowing she was nothing more than a money-hungry, horny, hood-rat.

Demetrius had just called Kamil and told him he was on his way. Driving on the freeway, he talked to Kamil on the cell phone about the incident that took place at the beach party between the Crips and Bloods and all the females' phone numbers he'd come across but never mentioned how Charles flat lined some thugs on Rosecrans with his P-94 Ruger out of his low-rider.

Before Kamil was finished bagging up his last ounce of marijuana, Devonaue's twenty-year-old little sister, Tasia, came through the kitchen door, walking in on Kamil which he was laying his last piece of marijuana bud on top of the small digital scale. Her eyes got as big as golf balls when she looked at all of the plastic bagged ounces of bright green weed lined up in rolls of ten.

"Damn, nigga. Let a bitch get a free bag of weed to smoke, K-Hog."

"Where your sister at?"

"She should be back soon with your grandmother. Last time I talked to her they were at Taco Pete buying some food." She started giggling.

"What the fuck you giggling for girl?"

"Nothing at all, but are you gonna let me get the bag or what, nigga?"

Kamil swung Tasia's five-foot-seven, thirty-four/forty frame around and slapped her square on her ass.

"Let me hit that young pussy, girl."

Tasia put her hands on her hips. "If I let you fuck, you can't tell nobody. Especially Devonaue and you gotta take me to a room, nigga."

"Yo sister ain't my bitch, fool. I'm a 'G' and I fuck who I want to fuck!"

"Well you better hope my sister don't pass that test or else you gonna be a 'G' with a crazy ass baby momma and a bad ass son."

"Fuck you, bitch, I ain't smoking shit with you, cuz. You trippin."

Devonaue was at the paternity clinic to see if Kamil's DNA was a positive result on her nine-year-old son, Vontray. Kamil's grandmother, Rita, rode to the clinic with her to make sure no schemes or lies were being formed even though the little boy looked just like Kamil, nineteen years younger.

On this specific day, a handful of Devonaue's female cousins and sisters were all hanging out at her house, waiting on her to come back with an answer like they were sitting around waiting for a new black president to get re-elected, campaigning on hood gossip, having worthless conversations in the living room about who's balling and what nigga is trickin' or spending their welfare EBT card on new designer clothes, and every last one of them sported gold from the swap meet with a weed or cigarette habit, popping ecstasy between. Indeed, yes they were beautiful black women, but were lost mentally from the lack of knowledge of whom the original civilized black woman was before the media and white materialized America deceived and destructed the black woman's true beauty which was her inner self and the way she conducted her behavior patterns. Our black female ancestor's like Harriet Tubman and Queen Asanti would be rolling around in their graves now to see how these hood rats gained a feeling of joy out of their urban fantasies and illusions.

Kamil swaggered through the living room after bagging up his weed in the kitchen, walking past Devonaue's family who were a group of females slouching around in the living room eating fried chicken from Popeye's and watching Steve Wilko's talk show on television. He stepped outside on the porch, the sun shining on his face as he saluted his right hand over his forehead giving his eye contact a good view of his grandmother's house down the block to see if they made it back from the clinic. When he stepped down off the porch, his phone in his pocket rung. He dug inside of his pocket on the right leg of his gray Dickie pants, grabbed his cell phone and answered the call.

"Who is this?"

"What's up, fool? This your boy, Cartoon."

"What's up, Cartoon? I'm just trying to get one of those cakes to bake for my party, is the family bakery shop back open?"

"Hell yeah, Dog, that's why I called you, fool. Me and Pepe just came from Mexico with my uncle earlier this week. Where you at and when you trying to do this?"

"I'm in the hood on 118th Street, between San Pedro and Broadway. You'll see a white Escalade on thirty-one-inch rims posted in the middle of the block."

"Like that, fool? You doing too much, K-Dog. That's how I'm trying to roll."

"Man, stop bullshittin, Cartoon, and come through!"

Kamil was back in operation with his cocaine connect. He just thought about purchasing a kilo brick for the meanwhile, just enough dope to quench the smoker's thirst around his hood and get the clock back poppin' and then pass the torch to someone trustworthy and who has patience to sit in the trap house all night, going rock-for-rock serving all the dope fiends. When he slid his cell phone down in his pocket, Meech pulled up in the GS Buick Regal cruising up slow and rolling down the window looking at Kamil, laughing out loud at him as Kamil grabbed the passenger door and took a seat inside with the door still open by the curb.

"So what happen, K-Hog?"

"Man, what the fuck is so funny?"

"Did the bitch come back with the DNA test yet?"

"Oh, you trying to clown me, huh, my nigga? That's fucked up, but it can't be possible that little nigga's my son, because I only fucked the big booty, hood rat bitch one time and that was ten years ago. The day before we hit that check cashing lick."

"Nigga, that's all it take is one time and you didn't wear a condom neither! Fool, you out of pocket anyway for fucking the bitch bare back."

"Yeah, I know. Fuck it, cuz, I ain't trippin'. Say Meech, drive me around the corner to the store real quick, so I can pick up some supplies to cook this bird I'm about to get from my Mexican connect."

Kamil closed the door on the Buick and they pulled off, heading for the store and catching up on lost times through conversation, continuing where they left off when they were kicking it at Imperial Beach at the Crips and Bloods low rider peace promotion festival.

***

When Devonaue walked through the front door of her living room, everyone grew silent and nobody moved an inch, waiting for her answer to see if her third to oldest son, Vontray, was Kamil's biological seed. One of her younger sisters, Brazil, was the first to speak on the issue from the couch, smoking a blunt.

"So what happen, Devon?"

"Vontray is that nigga's son without a doubt, and I ain't trippin' because that nigga Michael can keep supporting him with his school clothes and kicking in money to a bitch when his check comes."

Michael was a low-level thug from the San Gabriel Valley area. He met Devonaue at a club and continued to fuck her without protection after their first night stand, being sprung by her head game of dick sucking and admired the way she fucked him. He was a sucker for hood rats, and gave her trap money on a regular and part of his checks from his job, trying to prove his fatherhood to Vontray to be valid, but even Vontray didn't respect him as his father because Vontray never obeyed him and never liked going with him, letting Michael know that their father and son connection was all about money and clothes.

***

Kamil walked out of Numero Uno Grocery Store holding a shopping bag and talking on his cell phone telling Cartoon where to meet him after Cartoon was in the area.

After they drove out of Numero Uno's parking lot, Cartoon was turning inside at the entrance and stopped on the side of them, rolling down the window on his driver's side, talking to Kamil while he leaned his body over Demetrius from the passenger's seat.

"Follow me to my grandmom's house around the corner, Cartoon."

Cartoon made a U-turn and followed them inside of his dark blue painted Super Sport Chevy pick-up truck with tinted windows. Cartoon made sure a bullet was cocked back in the chamber of his Desert Eagle, just in case it was a bad drug deal. Even though he had sold drugs to Kamil plenty of times, he knew of his stick ups in the past of other drug dealers who he robbed, and of other black's fucking off their trust within the Mexican Mafia's cocaine dealings with them as a whole (Crips, Bloods, Pirus, etc.).

An old looking ice cream truck bent the corner on 118th Street and Avalon, looking for some welfare money to be spent by the neighborhood kids. The truck drove slow as the fat old Mexican man behind the wheel of the truck noticed a group of little boys emerging from an abandoned house. Vontray was leading the six-pack of black bastards, holding a stick, wearing a pair of dirty Michael Jordan sneakers, black jeans and a dirty t-shirt with French braids going down both sides of his head with a diamond stud earring in his left ear, big enough to fit a grown man's ear. The kids crowded up to the side of the ice cream truck, gazing in through the small window on the side at all the snacks and toy guns. The driver was at the window asking Vontray what he wanted.

"Let me get some Nachos and three big sticks."

"Give me your money."

Another little boy wearing a black cap to the back ordered some water balloons.

"Okay, let me get your money first, last time I give you ice cream, you run with it!"

Out of nowhere, a water balloon filed with urine splattered across the metal bars blocking the window where the ice cream man's face was and the piss splattered against the chubby faced man. He yelled with anger, "Fucking negritos! Putos!

A hail of rocks and small handfuls of dirt was thrown at the truck by the misbehaving bastards as the truck drove off. The kids ran after the truck, continued throwing rocks and yelling out curse words. An old lady who was watering her grass across the street looked in awe and shook her head, laughing. Demetrius and Kamil saw the entire fiasco as they drove by the kids, turning inside of Kamil's grandmother's driveway.

"How's your grandmother doing, K-Hog?"

"Shit, G-Mom's is straight. She just getting old and tired. She don't go to church no more as usual."

Rita's house still looked the same from when Demetrius would spend nights and some weekdays after basketball practice with Kamil and Montreal. Kamil paid for the house's fresh coat of white paint, but other than that, everything was the same. The same huge oak tree in the front yard. The same white picket fence. The same ceramic birdbath with a statue of a squirrel that squirted water from its mouth.

Cartoon parked in front of the house and followed Kamil and Demetrius through the side of the house up the driveway, holding a car part box from AutoZone. Kamil still had his old sky-blue BMW parked in the back draped with a car cover.

"Sit it right there so I can check it out, Cartoon."

Cartoon opened the box and placed it on the hood of the car, pulling out the brick of cocaine and handing it to Kamil.

"Its pure cocaine, K-Hog, straight off the Mexican border from Sinaloa, fool."

Kamil removed the ceramic plastic from the brick, exposing a portion and licked it with his tongue. His facial expression became bitter looking as if he sucked on a green lemon fruit.

"Yeah, this some good shit, Cartoon. How much you gonna give it to me for, Loc?"

Cartoon crossed his arms across his black Los Angeles Raiders football jersey, contemplating his offer.

"I'll put it like this, fool. You can either purchase the last seven kilos I got left in the cut for a big deal of eighty thousand, when I really should be charging you one hundred and five thousand for fifteen a key or you can just give me thirteen for this one."

"So you giving me seven for twelve G's a piece?"

"Hell yeah, Dog. You getting a steal not a deal, especially when coke is short around South Central."

"Let me give you ninety G's in cash and throw this one in for free."

"Give me a even hundred and take all eight."

"Alright, Cartoon, I can respect that, homey. I'll give you twelve thousand right now for this one, then we can meet later and I'll get the other seven bricks. Let me go and get the money and I'll call you, but I got twelve on me now."

Kamil dug in his front pocket, pulled out a dirt folded wad of Benjamin Franklins, and broke Cartoon off his money for the single kilo he brought with him, and then he left out the backyard after shaking both their hands.

CHAPTER 24

The next day, Demetrius dropped off his son at his mother's two-bedroom apartment in a fourteen-unit housing complex in Hawthorne. Nassir held on to his bag of clothes, leaning on his skinny shoulder slumped over, while Demetrius banged on the front door. When Amber opened the door, she was wearing a pair of dark Prada shades, letting them both enter and then closed the door.

"Nassir, go to your room, baby, and play your game and let Mommy talk to your dad."

"Okay, Momma."

After Nassir wrapped his arms around his mom's waist, he left his bag in the living room and walked to his bedroom. Demetrius was standing in the middle of the floor, looking clueless in front of Amber. She was facing him, still wearing her shades with her left hand on her hip. He felt something was wrong with her when he heard Mary J. Blige playing low through her living room stereo system speakers, *"I can love you, I can love you better than she can."* Amber's number two classic song on Mary J. Blige's album, *Share My World*. She would always play that album when something was wrong or her feelings were hurt.

Demetrius smelled the strong stench of chronic weed and house cleaner as if she had just finished smoking a blunt.

"Amber, what up with you, something wrong?"

Amber took off her glasses and revealed Scrilla's handiwork. It was black and puffy with red lining.

"What the fuck happened to your face?"

Amber broke down crying and embraced Demetrius, sobbing on his long sleeve thermo white t-shirt, laying her head on his chest.

"They tried to kill me, Meech."

"Who! Who tried to kill you?"

Demetrius knew that he still loved his high school sweetheart because he was feeling her pain as if someone stepped on his toe with a fifteen-ton steel boot, feeling the connection through her nervous system.

Demetrius consoled her for a moment, rubbing the palms of his hands through her freshly pressed black shining hair and lifted up her face, looking into her hazel eye with the ugly mark around it.

"You ready to talk or not?"

"Your homey, Scrilla, tried to kill me and the bitch Stella who work for him tried to set it up."

Demetrius instantly grew angry with a murderous look on his face, a knot growing in his throat. He saw Nassir peeking through the doorway of the hallway.

"Go in your room, Nassir, we almost done."

"What's wrong with my momma?"

"She's fine, my nigga, just go in your room."

Demetrius called Khadijah from Amber's house phone and took a seat down on the beige leather double-breasted couch with dark brown pillows positioned in the corner. She answered her office phone on the third ring.

"Milton Grime's Law Firm, good morning, may I help you?"

"Hey Khadijah, this is Meech. I need a number on Scrilla, right now."

"Hold on, let me pull it out my phone, 310-555-8742. So am I'm going to see you soon?"

"Yeah, I'll call you as soon as I finish handling my business today."

Demetrius called Kamil as soon as he hung up the phone with Khadijah.

"K-Hog, what's up, cuz. Where you at?

"I'm on the eastside with Fat Mouse and a few homies at a meeting with these Piru Blood niggas that's trying to call a cease fire after that bullshit went down at the beach."

"Where y'all at? I need to come meet you."

"We at Enterprise Park on 131st and Central. Make sure you bring your strap with you just in case it get ugly because these niggas from Black-P-Stone and a few Bloods from Athens Park is here, but the Crip homeys from Carver park and Nutty Block is supporting us. Your Pop's here to. It's a little bit of everybody. The Rollin Crips, the Gangster Crips and the Compton Crips and East Coasts."

***

Compton City Detectives O'Miley and Sanchez were having a field day snapping multiple pictures of Crips, Bloods and Piru members from across the canal that separated Enterprise Park from Centennial High School. They were tucked away in the back of the high school inside of a FedEx company van with digital long view cameras. A couple units were driving up and down Rosecrans Boulevard, in the black and white patrol cars, waiting for the meeting to end and pull a couple of gang members over for no apparent reason.

Some Crips and Bloods were stopped by the police on their way to the park, harassed for nothing but the fact that they were acting organized, which was rare in Killafornia, which frightened the U.S. Government and secret society of elite white Jewish rule, who viewed the value of black street gangs coming together a dangerous movement.

By the time Meech made it to the cease-fire meeting, it was near a call to an end of the meeting. He was late because he had to stop by his mother's house to grab his 9-millimeter Berretta from his bedroom so that he wouldn't be riding solo. When he pulled in the parking lot of Enterprise Park, it was hard to find a parking space. Cars and SUVs were piled in the gate, lined up and cluttered outside the gate, parked on both sides of the street by the curb, from old school to new schools and a few Harley's and street bikes.

Demetrius began to look for Kamil's white Escalade and Charles' 1986 black Regal Grand National, while looking at the variety of models that consisted of Big Steve's cherry red Harley Davidson with a twenty-three-inch wheel in front, a black Harley with a brown Louis Vuitton seat with a chromed-out engine, a couple of choppers and racing street bikes, a few low riders, a dark blue '86 Cutlass on gold Dayton rims and hydraulics, jacked up in the air, a citrus silver '64 Impala on one-hundred-spoke chrome Daytons, a burgundy '86 Regal on twenty-four-inch chrome rims, an '86 two-door, two-tone black and gray Chevy El Camino sitting on deep dish twenty-four-inch gold Daytons with fat gold racing tail pipes and a gold racing steering wheel, a dark blue four-door 2003 Lincoln on chrome Daytons parked on three-wheels in the air, a 1964 convertible Impala with a candy color red paint, peanut butter leather interior and convertible top, dropped down to the parking lot concrete on a set of 13 x 7 candy red Daytons with red spokes and lips and a plaque in the back window that read out Damu Riders in all chrome, a black on black 1972 Chevy Chevette Super Sport sitting on twenty-four-inch Lowen Hart rims with two racing stripes going across the middle of the car, a couple of 745 and 750 BMWs, a candy blue Range Rover, and the list of vehicles went on and on as far as the monikers and nicknames of the documented and well-known gang bangers who drove them.

Before Demetrius exited the rental car, he tucked his pistol in the waistline of his creased black Armani jeans and swaggered across the parking lot in a pair of $900 black cemented style Air Jordan basketball shoes. He walked past a group of thugs draped down in all blue attire, noticing one of them, C-Loc and Bone from the Carver Park Compton Crips gang. He shook hands with them and they pointed toward the bleachers where Kamil was hanging out surrounded by a group of East Coast Crips from different sects and saw Charles in the middle of the field, standing chest-to-chest facing his friend from his old construction job, Big Steve, a Blood Commander from the Pasadena Devil Lanes. Big Steve had on a pair of suede red pumas, brown sagging Dickie pants and a white t-shirt with a dozen Bloods behind him, watching the number of Crips behind Charles, aka Big-C, who was draped down in a royal blue long sleeve Coogi sweater, royal blue Dickie pants and a pair of dark blue Nike Air Max running shoes. Charles took off his dark shades, looking Big Steve in the eyes.

"Look man, your little homie was in the wrong for shooting Fat Mouse in the leg over a fucking low-rider hop contest. Okay, Big Steve, two wrongs don't make a right, but from now on, my nigga, we gotta stop all the bullshit because we got too much on our hands with the Mexican gangs already."

"We'll see how long it will last then."

Charles and Big Steve shook hands while a mob of Crips and Bloods filled the entire park around the middle of the meeting with a massive amount of blunts being smoked and bottles of liquor being drunk.

Although a small level of peace was made, the Y.G.s (young gangsters), B.G.s (baby gangsters) and Tiny Locs still didn't understand the depth of peace and the power it withheld with the black man in America's ghettos as a collective force.

After a meeting with Charles about a caper that will fill his pockets until he came across employment again, Demetrius met up with Kamil in the parking lot. Kamil was leaning up against the back of his Escalade, talking to a group of thugged-out looking black men in front of him that were wearing blue except for one who sported a red LA Dodgers baseball cap, white t-shirt, gray Khaki pants and red Chuck Taylor's.

While in the Los Angeles County Jail for a year and California Chino State Prison for six months, Kamil befriended four gang members—Devious a Compton Crip, Bull Rock a Devil Lane Blood from Pasadena, Spooky Slim a LA Crip from 190th Street in Carson, California and Scatter Brains a Crip off the southwest side of South Central Los Angeles, which whom Demetrius knew from back in the day—notorious for their efficiency and intimidating presence throughout California jails and the streets. From this small meeting, Kamil had given birth to a crime clique called U-Mob known as Un-Forgiven Mobsters.

The moment the detectives and the three Dodge vans filled with FBI Agents viewed the two tribes making peace, they grew angry and disturbed about it.

Demetrius walked up to the group of plotters, greeting everyone with handshakes, and introduced himself as Meech Loco from the Westside Crips. He pulled Kamil to the side and explained what Scrill did to his son's mother.

"Yeah Meech, I heard about the incident, but it wasn't told like that. I ain't seen that nigga Scrilla lately."

"You wasn't fuckin' with him while I was gone to prison?"

"Fuck that nigga, he owe me $100,000 for killing this old rich white man for him. I found out that the nigga lied to me, saying the man ripped him off for a load of hookers that was being smuggled in from China. Come to find out, some other rich white muthafuckas he connected with paid Scrilla and his Jamaican relatives half a million to kill the fool that I killed, who was a dirty U.S. Republican, that was doing underhanded shit, like betting on presidential campaigns and stealing tax money from the U.S. Government."

"Damn K-Hog, that nigga Scrilla a foul ass nigga, and I didn't know he was deep in the game like that."

"This shit get way deeper than you think, my nigga. He been using us ever since we met him when he moved out here. The only reason he wanted us to go to the NBA was for him to find a spot to fit in the financial world on a more higher lever, hiding his face behind us."

"So that's why he was always giving our parents money to sign us up for basketball camps ran by NBA players and always looking out, huh?"

"There you go. It would have been a good thing if we would've made it to the NBA, but I got word from a ballin' ass nigga from the Mafia Crips on Main Street that he was being taught how to form a contract on our names as him being our co-manager if we would've made it to the NBA. I saw the whole blue print on how he was to do it, if he gave his crooked white Jew whose father is the owner of several NCAA teams, a quarter of a million."

"Damn, K-Hog, that's deep! I still can't believe it. I feel betrayed and stupid. I had mad love for cuz, then he just tried to kill my son's mom."

"Shit, that ain't it. The nigga losin' his street credit with a lot of hood niggas, giving out false promises, and he started off manipulating young gang bangers, paying for killings of other members to gain more weight when he used to sell dope. He ain't no gunslinger like you think he is."

"That nigga gotto go, K-Hog."

Before the day ended, Demetrius and the new crew formed a way to get some quick cash and he took his mom back the rental car, so she could return it to the company and then he spent the night at Amber's.

CHAPTER 25

The night of the cease-fire meeting at Enterprise Park when Demetrius got to Amber's house to spend the night, she never came home. He woke up to a call on her bedroom night dresser with the phone ringing at 4:00 AM. It was Amber's mom, telling Demetrius that she had to pick up Nassir from the police station because Amber had been arrested for DUI and possession of a firearm. Amber gave Demetrius the keys to her apartment the day he picked up Nassir and told him he was always welcome until he got on his feet financially.

Two weeks later, Demetrius received a call from Scrilla on his LG Flip cell phone while carpooling on the freeway in the backseat of a black XS BMW SUV. Kamil was driving and Charles was riding passenger while Bull Rock was on the side of Demetrius, swigging on a bottle of Thunderbird strong wine.

"Hello, who this?"

"Scrilla the Reala. What's good, boy?"

"How you get my number?"

"Come on, young Meech, you sounding like I'm your enemy, the man that paid for you to beat the system when they was gonna wash your young ass."

Demetrius put Scrilla on speakerphone to let everybody in the car get an earful of the conversation.

"First and foremost, cuz, I'm far from saving a bitch, but you foul for trying to dirt my baby momma."

"Look here, Dog. The bitch was hella out of pocket. She attacked me first and I ain't never tried to kill her. The gun was fired off to scare her away because she kept attacking.

"Cuz, you a lie because you told Khadijah that it was your bodyguard who shot the pistol, but we gonna call it even. I'm not looking for no beef with you. We come down a long road of loyalty and love and respect, cuz."

"I'm going to leave that false allegation alone, but Khadijah's foul. She just mad, because I don't want to get serious with her and go beyond business, so I fired the ho as my attorney and cut her off, but I'll get her knocked off for trying to break us apart."

"No need for that, cuz, she can't fool me. I apologize for jumping to conclusions."

"Man, my nigga, it's been a long time. The Feds been on my tail, so I been sticking and moving, so don't think I was on some bullshit, but peep game. I got about twenty-five racks to slide you to have some pocket change and we can hook back up and get shit right, and to make it better, I won't ever trip on Amber and the year she owes me on the contract. I got ten racks for her too. Let's make peace, Dog."

"I'm on my way to paint a house now, but when can we hook up?"

"When I get back from Cuba, I'll call you on this number. Oh, by the way, have you seen that nigga, K-Hog?"

"A few times, but he still wild and I'm too matured for all that; I'm trying to be on some player shit and take it slow."

"Say, Meech, that's on my momma, rest in peace. That nigga K-Hog's a bitch on the real, Dog. Stay away from that clown."

"What he do, Scrilla?"

"That nigga was rollin' with me one day and I let that nigga hold my Uzi while I made a purchase for a hundred pounds of Kush. The nigga let me get robbed by two niggas and they only had one gun and he didn't even bust while he was hiding in the backseat behind the tinted windows of my Benz while I was buying."

"Fuck cuz, then, but call me when you touch down in Cali, I'm at work."

Kamil was so pissed off listening to Scrilla lie on him, he had to pull off the freeway and pull over. Demetrius was also heated on how he lied on Khadijah and his baby momma when he sat in Khadijah's office and listened to her tell Scrilla she was through with him.

When they got to their destination, the four of them did a home invasion robbery on a group of black thugs in the valley who used a four-bedroom house as a safe house to stash tons of marijuana that was grown on acres of farmland in Fresno City that was big enough to fit the plants on two football fields. During the robbery, one of the victims tried to get bold and run for a shotgun on the kitchen table after Charles kicked in the front door yelling, "FBI, don't move!" Before the robbery was over, Kamil amputated the hands of all four victims after they were handcuffed and shot in the back of their dreadlocks. When Scrilla got the call and heard about his stash house being robbed, he knew he was being tested at the highest.

His brand new eighteen-wheeler freight truck was stolen and he was clueless about who could have committed the mob hit. Charles drove the freight truck back to Los Angeles, following the U-Mob boys in the XS BMW, which was loaded with three stolen AK-47s and five briefcases filled with massive amounts of mafia money.

The stench of the decomposing bodies smelled so bad when Mortimer walked in the kicked down door of the stash house, he shook his dreadlocks, pinching his nostrils and left before the police arrived, but he was the one who reported the mob hit to police from a public payphone.

While Charles drove the freight truck with finesse, he was told by Demetrius on his cell phone that it would be best to pull the truck through an open project housing where it was blocked off by any public viewing or main streets or roads where the law enforcement would stumble across it. By the time their caravan made it off the freeway, they all decided to unload the truck in the middle of the Nickerson Gardens Projects where Charles' brother, a known Blood shot-caller allowed him to unload the truck between four housing apartment buildings where he sold drugs from. Before going over there, Demetrius had picked up Charles' pick-up truck from his mother's house on the way, along with a car cover he snatched off Charles' Cadillac low-rider that was parked in the garage. Kamil drove the XS BMW back to Slauson Boulevard where Charles was standing by the freight truck, and they got back on the road, heading eastward to Watts, leaving from the wild west of South Los Angeles.

When they made it to Nickerson Gardens, Charles turned inside the project housing from a wide main street, Imperial Boulevard, comfortable enough for the freight truck's size to enter.

Everyone in the projects knew Charles' brother, Bobby, so

they were safe. They just had to keep an eye out for police. When they pulled up to the housing complexes, Bobby was watching them from out front, holding a muscular, black Pit Bull by a thick chrome chain, feeding the dog a piece of Kentucky Fried Chicken from the small box he was eating from. A part of him identified Charles, with his slightly protruding belly on his old muscular body frame and wide bubbly eyes, except he wore a small natural and was five years older than Charles who sported waves in his hair that were slightly shaded with gray from aging.

When Charles climbed down from the truck, he gave his big brother a tight gripped hug, after he tied the Pit Bull's chain to the street pole.

"Look at you, baby bro! You look good, Blood."

"Don't Blood me, nigga, you know I'm a Kiway!"

Charles playfully hit Bobby in the gut. Kiway (Kiwe) stood for Crip or Cripped in the African language, Swahili, a term that most gang members who were up in age or did long stints in prison used.

"So you ready to unload, Big-C?"

"Yeah. You got the U-haul ready?"

"Yep, it's right in the back of that apartment."

"Alright, let's get to business, Big Bro, and I'm going to

look out for you real swell."

Charles flagged his hand at the crew, telling them to get out the truck and meet his brother, Bobby, aka Bloody Bob, a reputable Blood gangster.

Bull Rock and Kamil exited the XS BMW and Demetrius climbed out of the pick-up truck, walking behind them. When they gathered around Charles and Bobby, Charles introduced them to Bob, letting Bob know that Demetrius was his stepson and Charles referred to Bobby's name as O.G. Bloody Sam from the Nickerson Gardens Bounty Hunter Blood gang, and Bobby banged on all three youngsters telling them to state their monikers and street gang they claimed before Charles walked to get the U-Haul to drive up behind the double back doors of the freight truck. He moved his right hand crumbling three fingers over his big black lips and whistled loud like a teakettle. Less than ten seconds, a little over a dozen rowdy looking project thugs draped down in all red and black attire emerged from Bobby's unit he controlled. Demetrius and his U-Mob crew watched the gangsters in red, with growing discomfort, and Bobby saw it on each of their faces and began to laugh.

"Y'all straight, Blood. Them the homies, they do what I say!"

When the Bloods came up to Charles mean mugging Kamil

and Demetrius because of their Crip tattoos, Bobby let his Indians know that the aliens were his relatives and to always give them a pass if caught slippin' in traffic during gang wars, playing his role as a righteous chief in gangland.

***

Amber was sitting on the bottom bunk inside of the Lynwood County Jail Women's Facility stressed out and keeping a close watch on all of the nasty looking women. Some were lesbians, bull daggers looking for a girlfriend to cuddle with or munch on while a few thuggish women roamed with only a handful of beauties like herself. She had been in for a week now and it felt like hell, wearing her blue jumpsuit every day that probably over a million women wore with a pair of white vans that were a size too big. While she was reading a book by James Patterson, a female walked up on her, catching her off guard to where Amber caught herself from attacking the female because of multiple proposals and ass pinching by bull daggers whenever she made collect calls.

"Hey, Amber girl, what you doing in here?"

"Girl, it's too much to tell. It's been hell."

Amber sat down the book and rose off the bunk, hugging Naomi. She was pregnant and her face was glowing.

"Girl who's baby is in you?"

"That muthafuckin' bitch ass Scrilla! I went to jail for busting the windows out of his Maybach at the club, now I can't even live here no more, Amber."

"What do you mean, Naomi?"

"I'm going to get deported back to Jamaica, because the police found out my passport was a fake," Naomi sobbed.

Amber held on to her as if Naomi were her child, feeling her pain and went on to tell her about why she was in jail.

"Amber Perkins, pack your things, you're getting released."

Amber heard her name being called over loud speakers in the two-hundred-body dorm and quickly gave her phone number and home address to Naomi and ran to the exit gate like a lion was after her.

CHAPTER 26

Scrilla had just gotten back from court two days after descending a 740 Jet from Cuba with Daniel Rockfort. He was trying to get custody of his fifteen-year-old daughter by a former stripper who worked for him in the past at the rise of his clubs. He had gone to court while Diamond wasn't present and spoke all kinds of lies, trying to make her out to be an unfit parent. Scrilla was growing frustrated each minute he drove away from Family Court. In the Hermosa Beach area, weaving from lane to lane inside of his silver and black two-tone painted Maybach.

Scrilla's rise in the streets has fallen and his businesses and financial connections were being divinely curtailed from lots of sides by the Game God of the streets for disrespecting and misusing his power toward hood niggas and typhoons who showed him nothing but loyalty over love even if they had to commit one of the worst sins to prove their submission to him and pay homage, but Scrilla was in the midst of Judgment Day in the city streets.

A town hall meeting was being held by crooked European leaders inside of a large public brick building located in an upscale Jewish community in mid-city by West Los Angeles. When Scrilla pulled in the parking lot of the chapel-looking building, he parked between a BMW 530i and a black Audi. When he gained entrance, after being searched at the door by two white men wearing business suits, he was exposed to a room full of power. Scrilla paused and looked around at all the eyes that were on him from the twenty men seated at a wide long table covered with a white silk cloth with wine glasses and cigar smoke filling the air. Scrilla noticed a few Jamaicans at the table mingling with the Europeans. Desi was seated next to Mortimer.

A ninety-year-old white man with thinning gray hair and a wrinkled looking face, wearing a black three-piece suit pulled away from the table and rolled his electric wheel chair on Desi's side of the table, looking at Scrilla then back at Desi.

"Who is this young man to you, Desi?"

"He's my nephew."

The old man looked at Scrilla, moving his electric wheelchair with a joystick on the right armrest and rolled the wheels of his wheelchair up close to Scrilla until he was smashing the top of Scrilla's black Alligator boots. The old man began to speak with a scraggly tone barely moving his lips and talking slowly while Scrilla towered over him, looking down at him.

"Son, do you know how much damage you have caused to my precious human trafficking business? Do you?"

Scrilla was quiet and Desi raised from his seat, walking up to Scrilla, and slapping fire from his face with his backhand, splitting Scrilla's left eye with a gold pointy nugget ring on his middle finger.

"Answer the man, you buffoon!"

Desi yelled so loud everybody in the room focused their attention on him, and then he slapped Scrilla again, as if he was a worthless bitch prostitute. Scrilla tried to stop the blood from trickling down the corner of his left eye, drying his wound with the cuff of his long sleeve button up black shirt, and then he began to stutter.

"No, sir."

The old man looked at Desi smiling.

"Desi, your nephew doesn't even know what's going on. He's dumbfounded, because of his actions with the American citizen negroid women that he has working with the immigrants at the businesses. They have showed misbehaving behavior and a couple of them are federal informants. I've invested a lot of money into the high maintenance strip club in Hollywood and in

New York, using my great nephews name to open the business, so how am I'm going to get my money back, Desi? Are you going to help your nephew?"

"Hell no! Where is all the money you made and Mr. Neil's share you were supposed to bring?"

"Someone robbed my house in the valley, Uncle Desi."

"Why did they rob it, you dumb bitch?"

"Because there were drugs that they were after."

"I told you, you don't need to use any drugs to expand you revenues, and you have gotten four of my loyal men killed, leading them into your ignorance. That house was supposed to be used for women only, to live and be guided about the business when they land from overseas."

Desi looked down at Neil.

"So how much does my nephew owe?"

Neil Steinburg chuckled at Desi, not about to take the bait after Desi told him at first, "Hell No," when Neil asked Desi was he going to help his nephew pay him back his investments. Neil tugged on his suit jacked and pulled a .357 Revolver, all chrome snub nose, from the inside of the coat and pointed it at Desi, pulling the trigger multiple times until the revolver was empty. Desi fell to the ground, clutching his stomach. The Jamaicans sitting at the table couldn't do anything about it, nor could Scrilla as he watched his uncle get gunned down by a senior citizen who was probably so weak that his only physical strength was only strong enough to squeeze a trigger, but his strength within the European English mob was enormous as well as his allies in other countries who benefited from the human trafficking business along with him. Desi and the rest of the Jamaicans in the hall raised their hands in the air as the two white men who were searching them at the door of their arrival confiscating their weapons, pointing semi-automatic weapons at them, along with a few men at the table, telling the Jamaicans to leave and go and get Neil's sixteen million dollars that was owed but stolen from Scrilla's stash house that Demetrius and his U-Mob clique found in the briefcases, along with the freight truck full of marijuana. Before the Jamaicans were escorted out and given warnings that their families information was recorded in their mob records, Neil shouted loudly from his wheelchair after lighting a Cuban cigar with his revolver on his lap and Desi's blood splattered across the front of his suit.

"No more niggers are allowed in my business from here on out, and the only thing black people are good for is basketball, run, shoot, and steal!"

Neil Steinburg and his European brethren laughed at his racist joke and continued to drink glasses of wine while Neil called his nephew, Daniel, on the phone and told him to have their flight on the jet waiting next week and a week was only given to the Jamaicans to return Neil's money.

***

The FBI had raided both Scrilla's clubs in Hollywood and in New York, rounding up over fifty women with at least ten who were U.S. citizens in each club, and looking for Daniel Rockford for questioning, because of the clubs being leased in his name along with the liquor license to run the inside bars. A month later, CBS News program, *60 Minutes* broadcasted the raid and exposed a bit of evidence in the case, which *America's Most Wanted* performed the same theory on its television show, with Scrilla's face plastered on the television screen, strongly suggesting him to surrender himself after a federal indictment warrant was sent out for his arrest from secretive informants giving information on him to law enforcement.

Scrilla was aware that he was on the run, but keeping in close contact with his cousin Mortimer and his Jamaican regime, the only small help he had left after getting his ghetto pass revoked by the Crip and Blood tribes in Los Angeles City, mainly in the South Central area.

He had already profited over twenty million alone that was given to Neil in the past from the money he was making off the women from the human trafficking business. Some of the women were good at other illegal activities that they were involved in, other than the sex and stripping business, which brought Scrilla entrepreneur money. One immigrant beauty from Puerto Rico was so educated she hacked in over ten celebrities personal information on their website after Scrilla sent her to a community college in Los Angeles to take up computer classes on the side of her work, using it as a cover up and a financial future tool as well. He made three hundred thousand dollars off her alone, not including the rich tricks that were doctors and lawyers.

CHAPTER 27

The Unforgiven Mobsters hit for a ton of Kush weed, which totaled one million dollars, with a Cali street price of five thousand dollars every pound they ripped Scrilla off for. The England mob money found in the briefcases was nothing more than bonus blood money that averaged up to eight million in cash. Kamil stuffed two hundred grand inside of the BMW XS. He flew his grandmother, Rita, to Alabama with one hundred thousand in cash to live with the majority of their family. He took over the mortgage to her house in the hood on 118th Street, kicking out his crack head aunt. He added another floor to the home and a big black steel gate in the front, and Pit Bulls roaming from the front to the back of the yard and video camera's hidden throughout the trees around the front of the house.

Charles and Vickie moved to a bigger home in a suburban black community located in Ladera Heights, further up west from their old hood. Bull Rock purchased a huge home in the

Pasadena Hills next to the Rose Bowl Stadium overlooking Pasadena City with his candy red 1964 Chevy on red candy spoke Daytons parked in the driveway behind a cherry red G.T. Bentley on chrome twenty-four-inch Asanti rims, living the bloody rich life with Red Nose Pit Bulls roaming the yard, and his brother, Ghetto Fox, helping him run a couple medical marijuana shops in Pasadena City and a skating ring for the community, which was raking in a lot of money, with a huge sign in from that stated: "No Gang Violence or Gang Attire."

Everybody in Watts was going inside of the Nickerson Garden Projects to buy weed from Bobby's spot after the U-Mob blessed him with fifty pounds of Kush, sitting him on $250,000.

Kamil "K-Hog" Brown was continuing to keep it gangsta and going hard on his ho baby mamma, Devonaue, with a bad ass beautiful sophisticated bitch he had living in Anaheim Hills, where he laid his head. Christmas was approaching and Kamil was in the hood putting his foot down at Devonaue's house in which he bombarded and transformed into a modern Sodom and Gomorrah with every foul bird flying in and out the cage.

"Clean this muthafuckin' house up, bitch! What's wrong with you? I got company coming through today and go grocery shopping for the house or something after you done!"

While she was laying on the couch in the living room, Kamil towered over Devonaue and snatched the blanket off her, and snatched the remote control from her, turning off the television

"Okay, nigga. Damn, I'm, getting up."

"Bitch, you better hurry up before I put my foot in your ass!"

Kamil was looking evil at her with a do-rag covering his braids, wearing a white muscle t-shirt, boxer draws and some black corduroy house slippers. He walked in the back room and sat at the edge of the bed, putting on a pair of jeans and white Nikes. Grabbing his cell phone off the bed, he made a few phone calls, setting up his business for the day.

"Hey, Big Steve, top of the morning, O.G."

"What's going on, K-Hog? You ready for me, young nigga?"

"Yeah, just come through around noon."

Kamil made a few more calls and while he was talking to Bloody Bobby, Tasia was laying under the covers. When she heard his voice, she pulled back the covers and tried to move his hand away while he was zipping up his denim jeans to pull out his penis, moving her face down and giving him a morning head job, sucking his dick while he talked on the phone. He gripped the brown Louis Vuitton head scarf as he shot warm sperm in her jaws.

"Don't let my cum spill on my jeans!'

Tasia swallowed every last drop and a knock sounded at the door.

"K-Hog, is Tasia in there?'

"She sleep! Go and clean up like I told you!"

By the time Devonaue shoved the door open, Kamil was

walking past her carrying a couple of kilo-bricks inside of a shoebox. She looked at Kamil and rolled her eyes because she felt that he had been sneaking, fucking her little sister from all the free sacks of marijuana he was giving her from time to time.

***

Demetrius witnessed his new rebirth in the City of Angels, more like the City of Demons, in Los Angeles City. He learned a fundamental lesson—access to money and resources is severely limited in the hood. He knew a true hustler had to transform every little event and every trifling object into some gimmick for making money. Even the worst shit that happens to you can be converted into gold if you are clever enough and he found that out in prison by educating himself through reading material.

Since the robbery heist they pulled on the Jamaicans, Demetrius was spending more quality time with Khadijah after she and her husband officially divorced. He had just left his mother's new home visiting his little sister Dominique who was at home from a war she was drafted to fight since the day he went to court and took ten years and occasionally he was in prison, Dominique drove up to Folsom with Vickie and Nassir.

"Baby, I'm on my way, okay?"

"Alright Daddy, hurry up! I miss you honey."

Demetrius closed his flip L.G. cell phone, hitting the gas on his new 2013 Jaguar Coupe. The paint on Demetrius' Jag was sprayed with six coats of glossy emerald black, black "Bliss" customized twenty-six-inch rims and Perelli tires, bullet proof windows, a back-up safety camera by the trunk as if it was a small key hole that was intergraded into the dashboard monitor that was converted for video viewing on the DVD satellite Alpine television that popped out of the dashboard and an electric firearm stash spot was built in the interior good enough to pass a search by the Sheriffs or LAPD. The U-Mob was born to live and die for material things!

Khadijah finally allowed Demetrius to know where she lived before they would meet at places like the Cheesecake Factory or her Law Office or a high-end motel in Malibu City of Hollywood. Demetrius got off the freeway, sliding his Jaguar through Rancho Cucamonga, California, mixing in with the rich white folks on every main road he drove down. He even nabbed a phone number from a blonde headed white woman that pulled on the side of his Jaguar at the red light sitting in her Rag G.T. Bentley wearing a pair of dark Prada shades. The first words that shot from her mouth were, "I would love to stuff your black cock down my stocking for Christmas." She had Demetrius feeling real bossy by the time he made it to Khadijah's place.

Demetrius slowed the speed down looking for Khadijah's address. She was on a street that seemed quieter and less cluttered than the other area he had driven through especially in Los Angeles when he spotted the four-digit numbers on the curb. He backed up and parked out in front. He removed his 9-millimeter Smith & Wesson from his stash and got out of the car. Walking up the walkway, he looked up at the building in front of him. He saw a five-story house that was only four windows wide. It has a beautiful town house, with a tall staircase leading up to a door with a fan light over it. A wisteria vine growing up the left side of the house all the way to the roof was covered with purple buds just about to burst into bloom.

Demetrius pushed the doorbell, and then waited. There was no answer. Even after three rings and fifteen minutes, there was still no answer. Demetrius looked to the side and noticed another door that led into the house. Going down the stairs to the ground floor door was a small box with a red bow tied around it. Demetrius started toward the stairs, but just as he was about to round the corner, he felt a heavy piece of metal touching the back of his head and blinked.

"Boom! Got ya!"

Demetrius turned around after hearing Khadijah's voice, giving a look of disbelief for joking with his life."

"I'm sorry, Daddy."

She wrapped her arms around his neck, kissing him in the mouth, letting their tongues wrestle.

"This house is proper baby."

"You like it?"

"I do like it. It feels peaceful."

When he grinned, Khadijah handed him the small box with the bow and he opened it, revealing a set of keys.

"What's this?"

"It's your birthday gift."

"What is it?"

"Keys to your new home."

"This one?"

"Yes, and when you're ready, move in, but you can keep the keys. There's no rush. I know you like running those filthy streets like a boy."

Inside, Demetrius followed her upstairs to the first room. A dark green leather couch was placed at an angle to a green marble fireplace, with two big comfortable looking green stripped suede chairs across from the couch. All of them sat on an oriental rug, hand woven in colors of green and cream.

"This is a meditation room I made for you, Meech, to smoke your weed or read or whatever."

She showed Demetrius around the entire house and made it to the living room where pieces of dark mahogany furniture and several framed photos of her family—her mother, her parents together, her daughter and herself from infancy to one year ago. Demetrius smiled when he saw a framed picture of himself with his shirt off in his prison jail cell from when he'd text Khadijah a picture and she got it printed out and framed.

"Our bedrooms are through here."

As Demetrius walked behind Khadijah, he watched her forty-inch hips sway in a pair of tight white Fendi jeans, gripping her firm lifted butt. She had her hair in a signature bun with bobby pins going through to stop her ponytail from falling and a pair of white suede open-toe Jimmy Choo heels revealing pretty, oily feet with white painted toenails and a white long sleeve cropped Fendi shirt. She took off her white framed Fendi glasses when they entered the bedroom.

In the bedroom the walls were painted dark green, the windows leading onto a balcony were hung with curtains of green, and baron striped heavy cotton velvet. The bed was a four-poster with no canopy and the linens were printed with Fendi symbols. Demetrius saw Khadijah lovingly run her hand over the comforter. She wanted him to stay for the night. Looking at her on the bed, she stripped and helped him strip from his birthday suit that consisted of a brown Louis Vuitton sweater with black denim jeans and brown Louis Vuitton Air Force Nikes with a white t-shirt and Louis Vuitton baseball cap.

She moved at a quick pace, unzipping his pants and jacket. The next moment, her hands and mouth seemed to be everywhere on him, tasting his cocoa buttered brown skin. Licking, sucking and clawing his tattooed back while he was smashed down on top of her letting his ten-inch thick rounded circumcised dick power drive in her pussy, swelling her lips up and knocking on her ovaries. He was startled by her, startled by sheer hunger, then his mouth was on her, breathing heavily and grunting while she moaned loudly.

"Ooooh, aaah, fuck me, Daddy! Oooh, my pussy is so fuckin wet!!!"

Demetrius's balls could be heard slapping against the cuff of Khadijah's round ass, he was hitting her so hard, responding to her with the same need that she was exhibiting. The expression on Demetrius' face was of desire and longing and need... caring...he looked like she felt, understanding her thoughts, Demetrius said, "I love you, Momma," and pulled her head back after she raised up, grabbing a handful of her hair after her bun came loose and pulled her head back to apply his teeth and lips to her throat like a vampire, sucking her soft spot. When he picked her up to ease her down on his manhood, Khadijah nearly cried out, but she wrapped her legs around his waist, locked her ankles and hung on as he pounded into her, with her back against the wall. Stroke after deep, deep stroke, she held on, her nails piercing into his back, her mouth sucking on whatever part of him she could reach.

When he finished and gave her one last thrust before limply collapsing against her, his head resting on her shoulder, she hugged him, pulling away from her. Demetrius looked into her face as though searching for an answer.

"Meech, I'm so sprung on you!"

Very gently, he kissed her breast.

"You like that, my black queen?"

"Yes, yes, very much."

Kissing her, he ran his hands over her soft thighs past her red rose petal tattoo and kissed her softly. They went on and on until four in the morning, falling asleep on the bed stretched out naked. The dim lamp was still on in the room with music by R&B artist Drake pumping low on the clock radio on KJLH. The lamp made Khadijah's honey-colored skin glow with Demetrius full long nude muscular body and dick resting beside her. He was the most perfectly formed man she'd ever imagined. He was Denzel in his youth…guys at the gym…he was a movie star.

The next day, Khadijah woke up while Demetrius was asleep and cooked him breakfast in bed—pancakes and turkey bacon. She grabbed both of their guns from the floor, her 380 and his Smith and Wesson 9-millimeter, and put them next to each other on the night dresser by the lamp.

CHAPTER 28

Kamil was posted in the front yard watching his son, Vontray, play with his friends in a game of football in the middle of the street. Ten minutes later, he heard a loud motor clapping and echoing through the neighborhood while Cartoon stood next to him in the front yard. Fat Mouse came up the block kicking gears on his black Harley Davidson with Big Steve behind him on a red Harley, kicking gears behind Fat Mouse with a pair of high top red Chucks Taylors and a red flag hanging out his back right pocket while Fat Mouse wore a blue flag flying against the wind out of his left. The kids crowded around the glossy motorcycles as they parked in the front of the yard. Cartoon shook hands with Kamil and left. Then Fat Mouse and Big Steve followed Kamil in Devonaue's house.

When they got inside, Kamil showed them two plastic-wrapped bricks on the glass table in the living room. Fat Mouse picked up one, inspecting it.

"This some good shit, young homey?"

"Hell yeah! Ninety percent cocaine. Pure!'

"How much can me and Big Steve get both for?"

"I'll give y'all two for ten thousand a piece since y'all working together."

"Good looking, killer, we will take both gladly!"

"What you and Big Steve up to anyway?"

"Big Steve got a area out of town that we can take over and sell dope. He's gonna send a group of rowdy Blood niggas out there to bully a few blocks and I'm going to send a few little Crip homeys and home girls to rent the spots out in Kansas City, Missouri."

"I can dig it. When y'all need more work, I'm the man to see now."

Kamil tossed their kilos of cocaine in a shopping bag from Neman Marcus and they left looking like twins wearing identical black leather Harley Davidson vests.

The U-Mob had gained stripes like the U.S. Army selling weight and doing respected business with different street organizations like America did with other nations. Kamil and his crew were communicating in essential ways with other crews of thugs, making their business swell.

Kamil was talking to Demetrius on the phone, walking in the kitchen to see how Devious was coming along with his Chef skills over the stove. Kamil told Demetrius to come by the spot when he made it back in Los Angeles then sat his cell phone down to help Devious cook up some dope which Devonaue and her sisters were ordered out the house by Kamil earlier to go out clubbing and find some trick ballers that could be robbed. Kamil gave them an ounce of weed for Christmas and money to buy top-of-the-line women's attire. They all loved K-Hog, the shit talking, disrespectful gangster because he kept all their kids in new Nike sneakers and kept the bills paid when before he wasn't coming around. The lights and electricity would be off from time-to-time and the kids would be munching on Top Ramen Noodles and hot dogs. They wouldn't think twice about setting Kamil up to be robbed because they knew that their lives would be tampered with, plus Kamil introduced them to a few street hustlers to help the hood-rat bitches eat without starving and keep a little currency in their purses that they could call their own. Without sucking and fucking for it or waiting to the first of the month. Kamil loved lying in a house full of hood rats, because he could stick dick in all of them with no problem and have his way whenever his square bitch would cause him to get mad and leave her, and venture back in the hood where he loved to be.

"Hey, what y'all doing, Daddy?"

Kamil and Devious was in the kitchen cooking dope when Vontray and Tasia's son popped in through the doorway wearing their new Christmas clothes early and fresh design braids with little gold necklaces that Kamil got them. Tasia's son was a year younger than Vontray and they both liked to scrap with other kids in the neighborhood and steal bikes. Kamil knew they were thug babies and Jesus couldn't reform the little bad motherfuckers into civilized kids.

"Go and grab two of your momma's head scarves out the room, Tray, and bring two milk crates off the back porch so I can teach you and Ely how to be ghetto superstars.

Kamil removed the plastic from a kilogram brick of cocaine on the kitchen counter next to the sink, while Vontray and Ely stood on top of milk crates on the side of him with Louis Vuitton scarves tied around their noses and mouths cowboy style to block too much of the cocaine fumes from going in their lungs. Kamil and Devious wore blue flags on their faces and Devious was behind them standing over the stove, with an empty mayonnaise jar and a box of baking soda beside a pot over the fire.

Kamil removed 125 grams (an eighth of its total weight) from the kilo, talking to the delinquents step-by-step as they asked questions interestingly and paid close attention. The weight was then replaced or cut with a filler or comeback. Both the cocaine and filler, typically a liquid additive called pro-scent, were thrown into the food processor that Kamil had on the counter, plugged into a socket, next to his L.G. cell phone that was charging. He blended the liquid in the food processor, telling them to pay attention, as he thoroughly blended it. He then grabbed Vontray's small hand, making him pick up the spatula to spoon the mixture into a mold.

"Let me do it, uncle."

"Next time Ely, it's your turn, but watch boy!"

"Okay, uncle."

Finally, Kamil had a five-ton hydraulic jack and pressed the kilo back together. By the time they had the kitchen smelling like dope, Demetrius and Scatter Brain was let in through the front door by little Ely. For every seven kilo that was cut like that, a new free one was formed, is what Kamil told them. Demetrius looked at Scatter Brains, shaking his head.

"This nigga, K-Hog, done lost his mind. These little niggas going to the Feds!"

Everyone in the kitchen began laughing loud and then they emerged in the living room, lighting up big blunts and drinking on Patron.

Kamil disappeared from the house, returning fifteen minutes later through the back door, holding a large green duffel bag that said, U.S. Army on the side, dropping it in the middle of the living room floor. The bag made a loud, plank, as if huge metal were piled on top of the other. The living room light was dim from all the thick clouds of marijuana smoke floating around the top of the ceiling.

Vontray and little Ely were sitting Indian style on the living room floor in front of a thirty-two-inch plasma television watching *Menace II Society*. Kamil unzipped the bag and removed powerful artillery. He took out a big black .45-caliber machine gun with a hundred round drummed clip, then a Carbine I-5 with a hundred round clip extended, a Mac-11, a Mac-90 and four Desert Eagle Pistols with red beam lights attached.

Demetrius picked up the .45-caliber machine gun, glorifying the deadly weapon.

"Where the fuck you get this from, K-Hog?"

"I got it from breaking in a house a long time ago when you were locked up. I robbed a bank in Frisco with that muthafucka! That's how I got the Escalade on thirty-one inches."

Kamil boasted proudly about his 211 in front of the U-Mob boys as they began to have a conversation about preparing for a possible war with the Jamaicans and Scrilla and breaking bricks of cocaine to make it snow in Los Angeles, clearing up the drought weather from Cinco De Mayo.

By the time everyone left, Demetrius was last to leave talking to Khadijah on his cell phone. While Kamil was sitting beside him on the black leather couch, chopping down cocaine rock pebbles with a razor blade, passing out free gram sized rocks worth $25.00 to all the smokers in the neighborhood for Christmas, letting them know that the first one was free, and to invite all friends and family who weren't snitches. Kamil's crack head aunt, Ruby, had brought most of the customers by and they were treated well and promised to be Kamil's new customers from here on out while he also passed out plastic cups of eggnog mixed with Hennessey along with the dope fiend's free gram.

When *Menace II Society* ended, Ely and Vontray were given plastic gloves to help Kamil bag up grams inside of small plastic Zip Loc baggies. He was introducing his son to a criminal way of life while Demetrius was shielding Nassir away. Ely and Vontray had already been to Juvenile Hall Jail anyway for snatching purses, because they were hungry, so Kamil felt he might as well teach them how to thug the right way and get money at an early age. Before Demetrius got up to leave, he slapped hands with Kamil and the thug babies.

"Say, K-Hog, you still be fucking that bitch, Diamond, who used to work for Scrilla back in the day?"

"No, but I saw her at the Fox Hill Mall with Stella last month. A girl was with them that was supposed to be Scrilla's daughter by Diamond. Them hos was on me and the homeys. I was going to follow Stella and pop on her for what she tried to do to your son's mom, but the police was three cars behind them when I left the mall, following them on Slauson Boulevard."

"Which one is Stella, I forgot how she looks?'

"She's the one who used to work at Scrilla's old strip club that had Gangsta Bitch tattooed on her ass."

Demetrius left and the smokers continued to exit in-and-out the house, letting Kamil know what all gangs were trying to sell dope nearby, so he could drive by and shoot up their dope houses out of business. The fiends loved Kamil and was happy to be a customer of his and a friend of his Aunt Ruby's.

The business side of hustling was relatively easy to figure out. It was the people, the various actors in the game, the rival hustlers, the big time dealers, the police who could be tricky, but strangest and most impenetrable of all was the world of the drug users themselves, the clientele upon which Kamil's business was going from dependent to independent over one night.

The smoker's behavior could be erratic and even downright frightening because a lot of them were former gang bangers who would rob your spot and kill you without a doubt.

With rival hustlers and the police badgering Kamil weekly in the hood, Kamil could get inside their way of thinking, because they all operated with a degree of rationality, but the drug fiends seemed to be dominated by their needs and they could turn unfriendly or violent at any moment.

When Demetrius climbed in his Jaguar, he received a picture text message on his screen; it was a horrific photo of his mother hog-tied to a wooden floor butt-naked with Scrilla pumping his long dick in her mouth while she cried. The text message read: *The secrets of war has just begun, Rookie. I need twenty million in cash and Khadijah to represent my case. I'm on the run! Contact me soon, your best way!*

The End

COMING SOON...

Young and Reckless

Part II